Pulphouse
FICTION MAGAZINE

Issue Thirty-One

Magazine Editor
Dean Wesley Smith

A WMG Publishing Magazine

Pulphouse Fiction Magazine Issue #31
Published by WMG Publishing Inc.
Cover and interior design copyright © 2024 WMG Publishing Inc.
Cover art copyright © grandfailure/Depositphotos
Small creature we call Thumper copyright © beutoszig/Depositphotos

Pulphouse
FICTION MAGAZINE

TABLE OF CONTENTS

Pulphouse Fiction Magazine
A WMG Publishing Magazine

Editor
Dean Wesley Smith

Executive Editor
Kristine Kathryn Rusch

Director of Operations
Stephanie Writt

FROM THE EDITOR'S DESK
AN EVOLUTION

The early years of most magazines are evolutions as everything from content to design and size and layout get tweaked in small ways some cases and majorly changed in others.

Pulphouse Fiction Magazine has got to hold the record now for surface changes in just thirty issues.

What we have held steady is our focus on top-quality stories that break through normal edges and pay no attention to any genre line. That has not changed.

But wow have other things changed on the surface over the last years since we launched in 2017. We went from a 7 inch by 10-inch size to a regular book size of 6 inch by 9 inches.

We started off quarterly with about 70 stories per year, moved to every-other-month with about 70 stories per year, and now have settled on our original goal of being monthly with 100 stories per year.

We started off with all kinds of ads and fun cartoons. The issues looked fun to page through. We made things less busy after the pandemic, then when we went to a monthly schedule, we went to basic plain look with just the stories to make sure we could hit that schedule.

We can hit monthly, and we proved it through all sorts of ups and downs.

So now, as of this issue, the fun look is coming back to the pages of this magazine. It might not be everything we are planning on doing later in the year and next year, but it will be a lot more than the last issue by far.

And now *Pulphouse Fiction Magazine* has its own store where you can get back issues, any of the 24 Pulphouse special collections, and also some really fun merchandise that fits the magazine and the new fun look.

So again, while keeping the focus on great fiction and

diverse stories, we bring back some of the fun that just felt missing over the last half year.

I really hope you enjoy the new look and more importantly the stories this issue. And every issue.

DEAN WESLEY SMITH
LAS VEGAS, NEVADA

KEVIN J. ANDERSON

Kevin J. Anderson returns for the 14th time to these pages with a really fun and original Dan Shamble Zombie PI Adventure. Of all the ongoing characters being published these days, Dan Shamble fits Pulphouse the best.

Kevin has published more than 140 bestselling novels and with his wife, bestselling writer Rebecca Moesta, founded Wordfire Press.

Kevin is known for Star Wars, X-Files, *and* Dune *novels, as well as his many original science fiction novels. But back in 2012 he started something a little different for him, a series of humorous horror mysteries featuring Dan Shamble, Zombie P.I.*

I love the fact that we have Dan Shamble in these pages.

HAND JOB

A DAN SHAMBLE, ZOMBIE P.I.
ADVENTURE

KEVIN J. ANDERSON

1

In the Unnatural Quarter, all the monsters and mythical creatures want to tell their life (or un-life) story: from werewolves spinning a hairball of a tale, to ghosts waxing spiritual, to vampires with a pointed biography.

But when a disembodied crawling hand, C.H. for short, decided to write his tell-all memoir, communication proved difficult. Still, at Chambeaux & Deyer Investigations, we were happy to help.

The precocious appendage entered our offices riding the back of a fat white sow, so I immediately knew the situation was well in hand. The pig prodded the door open with her nose, while the crawling hand gripped one of her ears between thumb and forefinger, in case the ride got bumpy. Behind them came a plump, smiling witch with an outburst of steel-wool hair under a pointy black hat adorned with stars and moons. The witch's long hooked nose sported a stylish wart, and her voluminous black dress smoothed and also widened her hips.

I had just emerged from my office, ready to don my fedora and wander the streets of the Quarter in search of mysteries, or maybe just lunch at the Ghoul's Diner. But I was always happy to chat with the Wannovich sisters.

"Mavis," I said with a grin on my cold gray lips, "and Alma! A pleasure to see you ladies. And C.H., it's been a long time!"

The disembodied hand twitched on the pig's neck, and Alma, the sow, reacted as if it were a back rub.

Mavis and Alma Wannovich were busybody witch sisters active in social circles around the Unnatural Quarter. They were both lonely spinsters and, like every human and unnatural, they wanted a little romance in their lives. Alma had once attempted a love spell from a popular manual, but the spell backfired due to an unfortunate typo, which irreparably transformed her into a large sow. Although Alma had adapted to her porcine circumstances, she and Mavis had sued Howard Phillips Publishing for failure to run a proper spell check. As a result, the Wannovich sisters now held senior editorial positions at the company, achieving some success with a ghost-written series of my fictionalized and occasionally ridiculed cases as "Dan Shamble, Zombie P.I."

Mavis cackled a greeting. "Mr. Chambeaux, while we appreciate your harrowing adventures, you'll just be a side story in our new epic autobiography of Mr. Crawling Hand, titled *Hand Out*."

Riding the pig's back, C.H. tilted onto his wrist stump to extend a forefinger, twirling it in triumph.

My beautiful ghost girlfriend Sheyenne rose up from the

receptionist's desk, sparkling and ectoplasmic. Most new clients react better to a sparkly, curvaceous, blonde poltergeist than to a zombie with a bullet hole in his forehead. "We'll help in any way." She beamed. "C.H. is an upstanding, five-fingered citizen."

I reached out to shake the hand's hand, which lifted him off Alma's back. "He certainly helped me out down in the sewers when we fought against Ah'Chulhu and his evil real-estate plot," I added.

As Mavis closed the door behind her, I set C.H. on Sheyenne's desk to give him more room to scuttle about. "So tell us about the project."

Alma bent her flat nose to the rug and snuffled around, grunting an explanation, which Mavis translated, "Mr. Crawling Hand came to us with a book proposal for his extensive memoirs. As a small, detached limb, he surreptitiously observed many important events, and he'll point the finger at some of the criminal activities he witnessed."

ON SHEYENNE'S DESK, C.H. fluttered his fingers, trying to communicate. It looked like he was playing a fast arpeggio on a piano.

Mavis's brow furrowed as she tried to make sense of the motions. "Ummm, he says it will be a sensitive story, compassionate, and very... touching."

"Will there be a digital edition?" I asked.

The witch gave a vigorous nod. "And a braille edition. C.H. has also agreed to do special signature sheets for us."

The hand scuttled across the desktop and picked up one of the pens next to Sheyenne's computer, proudly tucking it between thumb and forefinger as he pretended to sign his autograph.

"I can't wait to read it," Sheyenne said. "Do you need us to give background interviews and pertinent information?"

"So long as we don't breach any legal or ethical agreements." Robin Deyer, my firebrand human partner, emerged from her office. She was a beautiful African-American woman with large brown eyes and neat hair clipped back with barrettes. She wore a smart navy business suit and carried a legal briefcase under her arm, although I knew she wasn't due in court until tomorrow morning.

"Of course, Ms. Deyer," said Mavis. "Due to the privacy issues, we will only expose the juiciest parts to scandal."

Robin gave a satisfied nod. She has a warm heart and a legal mind like a steel trap. Ever since the Big Uneasy—the cosmological event that allowed all the mythical creatures to return to reality—she had set her sights on finding justice for the downtrodden, which in this case meant the various unnaturals for whom old human law did not apply.

While Alma snorted and snuffled, a shrill squeal came from the conference room, and our little vampire girl darted out, wearing her pink unicorn sweater. Her blond hair was in bouncy pigtails, and her baby fangs were a bright white against her lips. "Piggy, piggy!" My half-daughter Alvina had a special bond with the Wannovich sisters, particularly Alma, and she threw her arms around the sow's neck. "I'm doing homework about pig demons and frog demons. Do you want to see?"

Alma pricked up her ears, but Sheyenne said, "These ladies are here on business, honey."

I looked at her and shrugged. "You gotta admit, that's an assignment neither one of us can help her with."

The kid was excited as she led the sow into the conference room, where her homework notes were strewn across the table.

C.H., meanwhile, gestured wildly, raised fingers in a peace sign, then curled into a fist and rolled around before balancing himself on a pinky. Mavis looked confused. "Sorry, I can't tell what he's trying to say."

Robin leaned closer. "Ah, he's using standard GSL. I'm well-trained in unnatural sign language."

"What does the G stand for?" Mavis asked.

"Goblin, in most instances, although it's applicable to gargoyles, gremlins, ghosts, and garglebeasts, but it has recently been expanded for use by any unnaturals who have at least one hand." She nodded toward C.H. "There's a simplified version for people with tentacles."

Delighted that he could now be understood, the crawling hand made gesticulations, finger movements, the hang loose symbol, and death-metal devil horns.

"What he says is compelling and alarming." Robin translated as C.H. continued his silent soliloquy. "He comes from a broken home, a divided family. There's crime and treachery—and lots of sex."

"Sex?" Sheyenne's pale glow intensified as she flashed me a glance.

Alvina popped her head out of the conference room. "Sex?"

"You go back in there, kid," I said.

Alma nudged the little vampire girl back to the report on pig and frog demons.

The severed appendage pranced about, and Robin explained, "He says he has a lot to tell."

C.H. hopped down onto Sheyenne's keyboard, and his fingers danced across the keys. Along the bottom of her screen, which currently held an overdue invoice from a harpy who was suing her equally unpleasant ex-husband for unpaid child support, the hand typed, "It was a dark and stormy night, and all good hands were sound asleep on their velvet pillows—"

Then our door burst open, and UQPD cops swarmed in, led by Officer Toby McGoohan, my best human friend. "Halt! Police!" I realized this was not a friendly visit, though he smiled when he saw me. "Oh, hey, Shamble!" He seemed surprised to find me standing in my own offices.

C.H. froze on the keyboard, his first two fingers lifted in surrender. Mavis raised her hands after straightening her pointed hat. Robin instinctively placed herself between the police and our two clients, though none of us knew what this was about.

Snorting, Alma waddled out of the conference room with Alvina right next to her. The kid flashed a pointy smile at McGoo. "Half-daddy!"

"Hi, darlin'. Sorry to interrupt your homework." He pulled a folded paper from the pocket of his blue uniform shirt. The other cops with him—a vampire, a werewolf, and a pimply-faced human—had their guns drawn, pointing at some imaginary threat.

McGoo cleared his throat. "I have an arrest warrant for the appendage that goes by the name of Crawling Hand, AKA C.H. He's been implicated in a smash-and-grab robbery at an Egyptian antiquities boutique."

C.H. rocked back on his wrist stump and splayed his fingers, either in denial or surrender.

"I'm sure he has an alibi," I said.

"He was caught red-handed." McGoo withdrew handcuffs from his belt and clipped the silver bracelet around the end of the severed wrist.

Robin was indignant. "We'll get to the bottom of this, C.H. I will act as your attorney."

"Oh, that's nice of you," said Mavis.

McGoo picked up the crawling hand, but the handcuff fell right off the empty wrist. "No resisting arrest now! I've got you in my grasp."

C.H. was trembling. Still holding the cuffs, McGoo snatched up the hand separately as the other policemen retreated to guard the hallway.

2

While C.H. was booked and fingerprinted, then placed in a holding cell, I faced McGoo at his cluttered desk in the squad room, demanding to know details of the crawling hand's supposed crime.

In her ectoplasmic form, Sheyenne hovered next to me, just as worried. "You're sure you have evidence against this particular separate hand, Officer McGoohan?"

"Oh, it's this hand, all right. The night guards identified him from mug shots."

I pressed, "I want to know what he was accused of stealing."

McGoo contemplated a stack of forms and files on his desk and scooped it all into the trash can. "I still have even more paperwork to do at the scene of the crime, Shamble. Come on, I'll take you there myself. The evidence techs are still bagging and tagging. It's a mess."

I couldn't imagine that the clever, nimble hand would be involved in bloody work. "Is it a violent crime scene?"

"No, but the mummy proprietor is a very disorganized hoarder—you'll see what I mean."

Ready to go, McGoo tucked his blue cap over his short red hair. He grinned a lot, usually at his own inappropriate jokes, which had gotten him in deep trouble in the past. We had been close friends when I first set up my detective agency in the Quarter, and he walked his daily beat. We remained friends even after I was shot in the back of the head when a case of mine went sideways. I'd clawed my way out of the grave and started work as a zombie P.I., back from the dead, back on the case. My own cases frequently required the resources of the police department, and McGoo just as often leaned on me for off-book investigations.

Now he led me and Sheyenne at a brisk pace partway across the Quarter, then down a back alley crowded with boutiques and curiosity shops. Yellow crime-scene tape was draped around the front of Notions of the Nile, whose sign was decorated with hieroglyphics that looked suspiciously like Egyptian emojis.

Sheyenne flitted inside, passing through the crime-scene tape and wall to move among the crowded artifacts. McGoo and I followed through the regular door. Looking around, my ghost girlfriend said, "How would anyone find a specific thing in all this clutter?"

Gremlin evidence techs moved about using magnifying glasses and museum brushes to study mounds of artifacts, rolled rugs, vases, urns, tapestries, carvings, ashtrays, cat toys, pharaoh love seats, and macrame hangings. With my analytical detective mind, I classified all the items as *Junk*.

The gremlins darted from shelf to shelf, dusting for fingerprints. They took photographs with large cameras, then used their iPhones to click selfies in front of a display of "I ❤ Egypt" sphinx curios.

"Hey, careful with that!" cried a rattling, raspy voice, and the gremlin techs jumped, then chittered at one another. A thin, desiccated figure wrapped in dingy linen strips creaked forward, making insistent gestures with petrified hands. "Every item is categorized by rarity and discount code." He turned to McGoo with a whistling huff through his sinus cavities, as if blaming him. "I've been robbed, Officer! I'm already a victim—do not make me a victim again with your oafish incompetence."

McGoo lifted his chin. "I prefer to think of it as *exceptional* incompetence."

The mummy hobbled forward on rattling, bandage-wrapped legs. Seeing my fedora, he assumed I was a private detective of some importance. "My name is Akhenatenominimum. Or Tony, for short."

I was glad to know the short version. "Pleased to meet you, Tony." I grasped his hand, careful not to break any of the desiccated bones.

He turned his coal-black eyes to me, hoping for better service. "I was robbed last night! Come, look at my curio case with the most valuable items in my shop."

Tony creaked over to a nook near the front of the store. "Notions of the Nile caters to only the most discriminating aficionados of ancient Egypt."

Next to an antiquated cash register, a glass cabinet held items of exceptional value, including some rarities that were priceless (or at least, they had no visible price tags). The top pane had been shattered, leaving a wide, jagged hole.

"That severed hand smashed the glass with his knuckles and snatched my most valuable artifact! A precious rolled scroll from ancient and magical times, sealed in a bright green scarab case."

"And what was this artifact, Mr. Akhenateno—uh … Tony?" I asked.

"It was very valuable!" the mummy exclaimed.

"Other than that…" I prodded.

"It was sealed by incredibly powerful wizards of the Nile, written down from a revelation by the well-known pharaoh fitness expert, Na-Pu-Ko-Tak." He paused, as if waiting for us to be impressed.

"I've never heard of him," Sheyenne said.

McGoo shrugged. "My mummy knowledge ends with Boris Karloff and Brendan Fraser."

"Na-Pu-Ko-Tak wasn't all that well-known," Tony admitted. "But he was very smart and gifted in the dark arts. On that scroll, sealed for millennia inside the valuable scarab case, was written the *secret of immortality!*"

"Hmmm, it does sound like a powerful spell," I said.

Sheyenne looked around. "Are you sure it's not just lost in the clutter?"

McGoo crossed his arms over his chest. "We'll find it, sir. Our evidence techs are the best in the business."

From the other side of the shelves came a loud crash as a cat-shaped urn fell, knocking down piled scrolls and a set of matching Egyptian cigarette cases.

"We found fingerprints all over the place!" called out one of the gremlins. "Smudges everywhere. We'll identify 'em."

The other gremlin tipped over a rack of pharaoh-designed leisure suits. "That detached hand should've worn a glove."

If the fingerprints matched, C.H. would be in even more trouble. I knew I'd have to talk with those witnesses and get the full story.

McGoo tried to reassure the fragile mummy proprietor. "We already have the perpetrating limb in custody. Once we interrogate him, we'll learn where he hid that scroll with the secret of immortality."

Since Robin was the severed limb's attorney of record, and I was his zombie detective, we went to see the prisoner. We needed face-to-face time with the hand. My determined lawyer partner was already building up a five-point defense for her client. She had filed paperwork to get C.H. free on bail, but the UQ Police Department, not to mention the HR Department, had a strict policy against loose hands.

The cold austere cell in the back of the precinct building had cinderblock walls and a concrete floor. A scuttling hand could easily have slipped between the wide iron bars, but C.H. had been placed in a gilded canary cage that hung from the ceiling. The rest of the holding cells looked empty, although one apparently held an invisible man who had been arrested for indecent exposure.

C.H. looked forlorn in his hanging cage, but when he saw us, he waggled his fingers at us in a hopeful greeting. His knuckles were scraped, as if he had tried to batter his way out of confinement.

Robin stepped into the cell. "We're here to discuss your case. I promise we'll use every possible defense strategy to get you out of here."

"Robin even knows some underhanded tactics," I offered, taking a seat on the lone bench against the cinderblock wall.

C.H. rattled around inside the cage, gesturing and pointing in convoluted gestures, which Robin interpreted for me. "He insists it wasn't him. He claims he's been fingered for someone else's crime."

Sadly, I had heard such stories before, and so had Robin. I spread my hands. "But two witnesses identified you."

C.H. tapped his fingers in an insistent denial on the newspaper that lined the floor of the cage.

Robin interrupted, "Don't worry, Dan will verify their story. Here in the Unnatural Quarter, night security guards tend to blow things out of proportion."

"At least the ones who survive," I said.

C.H. made more urgent gestures, and Robin said, "He insists it's a case of mistaken identity. Many hands look alike."

"How many disembodied ambulatory hands are running around the quarter?" I asked

Robin pointed out, "They can't run, Dan—they're hands."

"Good point, but not the point."

The crawling hand gave a detailed, emotional explanation. Robin listened and watched, though she looked dubious, "He claims it must be his twin brother named Lefty."

"Lefty?" I peered into the cage. "So an identical twin?"

"Fraternal twins. They were separated at birth, but Lefty

has led a far more sinister life, crawling around in the seamy underbelly, sticking his thumb in the shadows. He has his fingers in every kind of black-market pie."

"That sounds suspicious—and also convenient," I said, looking at the abbreviated hand. "But you're a left hand. Are you saying your brother Lefty is the same?"

Through insistent gestures, C.H. explained that, no, his twin was the *right* hand, but had chosen his nickname strictly to confuse matters, proving how sinister he really was.

I was ready to begin my investigation. "Any idea where to find your brother?"

In a weird wobbling movement, C.H. made a thumbs-down gesture.

Robin wasn't discouraged at all. "You know that Dan is the best zombie private investigator in the quarter."

"It says so right on my business card," I said. "Zombies are relentless and persistent, and I never give up on a case."

I rose from the cold bench, feeling the stiffness in my knees. I needed to go back to the All-Day/All-Nite fitness center in order to keep the rigor mortis at bay.

A ghoul jail attendant opened the door and shuffled forward, carrying a tray of food. Though he wore a UQPD uniform, the gray-skinned, drooling unnatural had been assigned to administrative duty, since ghouls weren't good at high-speed foot chases or shootouts.

"Lunchtime," the ghoul said, dragging out the word like a dead body. He banged the tray against the bars of the cell. He used an iron key to ponderously work the lock, then swung the creaking door open. He shuffled in and dropped the tray on the metal bench far from the canary cage. I saw it was a special meal of hand rolls and finger food.

C.H. made listless, forlorn gestures, and Robin translated, "He says he's not hungry. He'll eat later."

We followed the ghoul attendant out of the cell. The barred door slammed shut with a loud, foreboding clang.

4

Since there had been so much chaos at the scene of the crime, I needed to have another look around at the Notions of the Nile.

"I want to go along," Alvina said with the boundless enthusiasm of an undead eight-year-old. (She was now almost twelve, but she had stopped aging after a botched transfusion infected her with vampire blood.)

"You'll get in the way," I said. From past experience I knew she would eventually talk me into what she wanted.

"But I'm your investigation research assistant. Pleeeease?"

"You'll poke around and go where you're not supposed to go."

She placed her hands on her hips. "That's what an investigation research assistant is supposed to do!"

She had me there.

Glowing, Sheyenne came up beside us. "Beaux, she could

use some fresh musty air among all the relics, and she'll get extra credit at the Nosferatu Academy."

I could never resist these two most important women in my life, and I knew when a battle was lost. "All right, kid, though I don't think Akhenatenominimum is the type of dried-up old soul to be impressed by cuteness and sweetness.

"But I'm so good at it," Alvina said.

That was another thing I couldn't argue with.

We set off for the ancient Egyptian boutique. Down in the shadowy back alley, with its drab awnings of various novelty shops, we came upon Tony peeling away the yellow crime-scene tape draped around his door. On a signboard, he had scrawled fresh words in chalk: "Today only. Post break-in sale."

Alvina said in a stage whisper, "He looks like his linen wrappings could use a wash."

The ancient bag of bones turned about with an indignant sniff like a hollow whistle through his sinus cavities. "They are *vintage*, young lady."

I stepped closer. "We spoke yesterday, Mr. Akhenateno-minimum. I'm Dan Chambeaux, zombie private investigator."

"Call me Tony. It's much easier."

"Akhenatenominimum!" Alvina said, showing off.

The mummy proprietor exhaled a long, dry sigh. "I'm just glad to get back to business. I've got a life to live, you know—and I've had one for thousands of years."

I tipped my fedora in a respectful gesture. "We'd like to ask a few more questions, sir, and have another look around."

Tony shuffled back into the shop, oddly unenthusiastic.

"The UQPD has the case well in hand. I just want this whole thing behind me."

"But we're sure they arrested the wrong hand!" Alvina said, bouncing after him.

Inside the cluttered Notions of the Nile, the stacked shelves looked as if they'd been ransacked. Clothes racks were toppled over, urns in disarray, sarcophagi half-open and filled with old magazines. I wondered if the gremlin evidence techs had caused this whirlwind of damage, or if this was just Tony's organizational system.

A piece of plywood covered the smashed glass top on the display case, but I bent down to look at the remaining valuable items through the side. "Are these other artifacts worth anything?"

Alvina wandered off to poke among the exotic items. She found a cartoon mummy Pez dispenser, but despite her persistent clicking, it was out of candy.

"You can see all the prices there," Tony said as he opened a ledger book and started to add columns. He seemed intent on ignoring me.

"Why do you think the alleged hand stole only the scarab case and not any of these other valuables?"

"It wasn't an alleged hand," Tony said. "It was a real hand. How else could it break the glass?"

"But why would it leave all these other rarities? Doesn't make sense."

The old mummy made another whistling huff through his sinus cavities. "He took the most valuable ancient scroll. How much do you think a single hand can carry when it's on the run?"

I repeated Robin's wisdom. "It can't run. It's a hand."

Still, Tony had a point.

I looked at the plywood top covering. "If that little scroll held the secret of immortality, why didn't anybody look at it before now? It's a pretty interesting secret. You'd think someone would peek."

"The coded hieroglyphics of Na-Pu-Ko-Tak are only visible under the light of an Egyptian full moon, which occurs rarely and unpredictably."

I nodded, as if I understood what he was talking about. "And what's an Egyptian full moon?"

"A full moon high in the sky covered by a veil of thin clouds, so that everyone sees it the way a mummy would look at it through gauze wrappings."

"Now it makes sense," I lied.

At one of the back shelves, Alvina stood on tiptoes to pull down a carved wooden box. She slid open the lid. "Look, half-daddy, I found a creepy dried monkey's paw!" She held the desiccated, curled thing. "I wonder what it's used for. I wish—"

I cut her off immediately. "Put that back, kid."

"But why?" She whined. "The discount says 'partially used.' What does that mean? I wish—"

"*Now*, kid! That's not part of the case."

With a sigh, the vampire girl tucked the shriveled monkey's paw back in its box and returned it to the shelf.

Even though Notions of the Nile had no customers, Tony was impatient to get back to business. "There's really no need for further investigation, Mr. Shamble."

"It's Chambeaux," I corrected, as usual.

"Everything is taken care of. I've already filed the insurance claim, and I have a very good policy that covers break-ins."

That made me suspicious. "But how do you place value on the secret of immortality?"

As he waved, Tony's gnarled hand looked remarkably like the shriveled monkey's paw. "They have adjusters for that."

As she rummaged among the canopic jars, Alvina found a small sarcophagus. "Look, it's a mummified kitty! Can I have a pet, pleeease? I've always wanted a kitty."

"Not today, kid." She had asked for a pet before, but Sheyenne, Robin, and I were worried that she wouldn't take care of it. Still, a mummified cat was lower maintenance than most other animals.

I motioned for the vampire girl to leave. "I'll follow up if I have any further questions, Mr... uh, Tony."

"Akhenatenominimum!" Alvina said.

"I am having a special post-burglary sale, Mr. Shamble," the mummy pointed out. "Surely you have loved ones with who are fond of old things?"

"My ghost girlfriend certainly is," I quipped. "But I'll have to be enough for her."

5

I arranged to meet the rent-a-cop Temporary Security Agency witnesses at a popular gypsy coffee cart. The gaudy red wagon was strewn with Christmas-tree lights and ornate colorful hexes. Hanging wind chimes tinkled in the breeze, accompanied by the hiss and snort of an espresso machine inside.

Two night security guards waited for me—a sleepy, pot-bellied human and his stoic golem partner, Bill and Urg. We had crossed paths before. Now, they loitered at the coffee cart, obviously waiting for me to buy. It was worth the invest-ment so I could get an honest report from them. Besides, the golem didn't drink anything.

"You two always find yourselves in the middle of dire circumstances," I said.

Bill shrugged. "We are night security guards around a bunch of monsters. It comes with the job."

Urg added in his deep, resonant voice, "That's why we get hazard pay."

While studied the lengthy hot drink menu on the side of the gypsy cart, I said, "I want to talk with you two about the Notions of the Nile burglary. You were at the scene of the crime when the display case was broken?"

"Yup, we saw it with our own four eyes," said Urg.

In front of us at the coffee-cart window, an Igor in a lab coat ordered a triple shot, half-caffeinated, extra foam, extra hot, dark-roast/light-roast blend latte with a caramel macchiato mark, double-cupped, and with a straw. Hearing the order, I knew I would have time for a long conversation with the two guards.

Bill patted his potbelly. "Urg and I were in the back, taking a careful inventory of the candy, snacks, and soda section when we heard a crash. We ran out and saw the hand right in the middle of the curio case."

The golem gave a ponderous nod. "Right there, before our four eyes."

Inside the coffee cart, the gypsy barista bustled around in a flurry of cups and measuring devices, pumping from bottles, stirring with a long spoon, and adding a hiss of steam. A bright red scarf was tied around her head, and her earrings jingled as she worked to prepare the high-maintenance order.

Bill continued, "I yelled for him to halt, but a hand doesn't have ears. The appendage kept doing his nefarious deed, and when I ran closer, he attacked me. That thing had a vicious thumb!"

"It tried to strangle him," Urg said. "Wrapped around his throat and squeezed!"

Swallowing hard, Bill rubbed his neck. "He had a real strangler's grip."

"But not much leverage," Urg said. "I was able to knock the hand back onto the counter."

Finally, the gypsy barista set the finished hot beverage onto the window shelf, and the Igor snatched it and departed without leaving a tip or even saying thanks. The gypsy barista leaned out and shook her fist at him, yelling a curse.

The Igor tripped on an uneven section of sidewalk and fell flat, spilling his drink.

When I stepped up to the window, the barista crooked a finger at me. She wore so many metal bracelets in a row it looked like a Slinky on her wrist. "You better not have a complicated order."

"Just a coffee, ma'am," I said and glanced at Bill.

"Large coffee," he said, "with cream and two sugars."

Knowing the barista was in a touchy mood, I dropped a five-dollar bill in the tip jar first, just to get things on the right foot. Mollified, the gypsy ducked back into the cart.

"Even after I knocked the hand away," the golem continued, "he grabbed that scarab case and scuttled off as fast as five fingers could go."

"Well," Bill said, "three fingers, because he was holding the stolen property in two of them."

"How do you know it was my client who committed this crime?"

"We saw him with our own eyes," Bill said, still sweating with his recollections of the ordeal from the night before. "Identified him from a mugshot. Crawling Hand. Unmistakable."

Urg said, "It was a hand job, all right."

While we waited for the coffee, Bill rubbed his throat again. "You can even see the bruises from when he tried to strangle me."

Indeed, the long purplish marks clearly outlined four fingers and the indentation of a thumb. As a detective, I held up my left hand, trying to match it with the bruise pattern. When I pressed it closer to Bill's throat, he flinched back, clearly not wanting to be strangled again.

But I spotted an important clue. "This isn't right ... I mean left. Look at the position of the thumb and the fingers. It's the wrong direction. My friend C.H. is left-handed, but these marks were made by a right-handed strangler."

Almost certainly one named Lefty.

Bill rubbed his neck with one hand, then rubbed it with the other. "You're right, Mr. Shamble. Was he maybe a back-handed strangler?"

"Sure looked like him from the mug shots," Urg said. "I

was never good at right and left." He glanced down at his shoes.

I knew I would have to investigate this further.

The gypsy handed us our cups of coffee, and we walked off, but the dark, bitter brew was no match for my thoughts.

Bill took a sip from his cup and let out a long sigh. "Good coffee. Almost worth getting strangled for."

"The police will want to question you again," I said. "You've been very helpful."

"We'll get around to it later," Bill said. "We have to be off now."

The golem nodded his big clay head. "Afternoon gig, guarding the toxic waste dump."

———————

BACK AT THE CHAMBEAUX & Deyer offices, I couldn't wait to share my strong new evidence with Robin—but before I could say a word, Sheyenne seemed just as excited to tell me about a discovery of her own. "Beaux, I ran a full search to find any evidence of C.H.'s missing evil twin!"

The little vampire girl bounced up beside my ghost girl-friend. "I helped, too! I know all sorts of interwebs tricks."

They were a great team. Sheyenne explained, "We searched for any evidence of loose hands or other single appendages in the criminal records, but C.H.'s brother is clean."

Alvina piped up, "Then we ran a search on the registered owners of illegal and black-market businesses, but we still didn't find any hand records."

They didn't seem disappointed at all. "That's a lot of things you didn't find," I said. "Why are you so excited?"

"Because Alvina suggested something that never occurred to me," Sheyenne said, and the vampire girl grinned, making her little white fangs protrude. "We looked for *legitimate* businesses owned by detached hands—and we found one!" With her poltergeist powers, she handed me a scrap of paper on which she had written a name and address. "And this is where you can find him."

In her office, Robin finished talking on the phone. She hung up and came out to join us, wearing a glum expression. And I hadn't even told her my good news yet.

"That was a disappointing call from the crime-scene lab," she said. "The fingerprints found on the smashed display case are definitely identical to C.H.'s. We'll never be able to prove he's not guilty."

6

I braced myself as I approached the shop door. A manicure salon, of course—Fancy Fingers. The chemical smells wafting out rivaled anything produced by a mad scientist's lab.

Inside, intense black lights shone down onto tables with finger bowls, rubber mats, and jars that held implements reminiscent of Nazi torture devices. An extensive rack of nail polish showed an array of colors like an apothecary's selection of deadly poisons.

Most of the stations were empty, but a hatchet-faced, severely beautiful Bride sat erect in a chair as a clumsy troll manicurist used thick fingers to rub lotion into the stitches that circled her wrists. Her Nefertiti hairdo had been done up to emphasize the white zigzag, and intense eyeshadow and lipstick indicated that the Bride was getting ready for a night on the town.

A second troll woman, obviously the receptionist,

lumbered up to me with a menu of services. "New customer?" She frowned at my grayish hands. "You need a lot of work."

"Self-improvement is on my To Do list." I looked past her to see the actual person, or partial person, I had come to see. "I'm here to speak with your boss."

On a purple velvet cushion rested a splayed, detached hand—a right hand. On either side, two pale vampire princesses caressed, massaged, and pampered Lefty. The hand relaxed on the pillow as the vampires kneaded his knuckles and fingers. Lefty's nails were perfectly manicured, as expected.

As I pushed my way around the troll receptionist, the vampire princesses looked languidly at me, their dark eyes like pools of night. They smiled like predators.

I stood before the purple cushion. "Mr. Lefty, I'm Dan Chambeaux, private investigator. I've been engaged to look into a burglary at Notions of the Nile."

Lefty tapped his forefinger on the velvet cushion, indicating disinterest. I continued, "Eyewitnesses saw a disembodied hand matching your description at the scene of the crime. Do you know anything about that?"

Lefty aggressively extended his middle finger at me.

In a sultry voice, the left vampire princess said, "We can translate for you."

"No need," I said. "The point was clear."

"Fingerprints at the scene have been linked to a client of mine, Crawling Hand." I leaned closer to the cushion. "But if you're his twin brother, wouldn't the fingerprints be the same?"

Chapter 6

Lefty extended his middle finger at me again, then added more gestures with his pinky and thumb.

"That's not how fingerprints work, Mr. Chambeaux," said the vampire princess on the right. "The prints on a left hand are not the same as the prints on a right hand."

"Ah, but not if they're twins!" I said, demonstrating my complete ignorance of forensic science.

"Crawling Hand is Lefty's fraternal twin, not identical twin," said the other vampire.

I seized on the little victory. "So you admit they're brothers!"

"Again, that's not how fingerprints work," one vampire princess said without even glancing at Lefty's frenetic gestures. The second princess added lotion to the back of the hand.

"It could be a genetic anomaly," I said, "or a plot contrivance."

"Lefty has an alibi for the night of the crime," said the first princess. "He was with us, giving a massage."

The second vampire purred. "He's very good with his fingers."

"Do you know anything about a stolen scarab scroll?" I pressed my bad luck. "The secret of immortality, written down by a famous pharaoh ... whose name I can't remember right now.

Again, the extended middle finger. Lefty seemed to have a limited vocabulary.

"What else can you tell me about your brother, C.H.?" I prodded.

Lefty just flicked his forefinger, as if snapping away an insect.

The receptionist troll loomed behind me, as did the manicurist troll. The two vampire princesses flashed their long fangs and held up their lacquered claws in a threatening gesture. Even the intimidating Bride had risen from the manicure station, upset with me for interrupting her beauty services.

"Well, I think that answers all my questions," I said. Inhaling a deep breath of the toxic nail polish and cuticle-softening fumes, I backed out of the Fancy Fingers manicure shop.

Hands down, that was a very uncomfortable and unproductive interview.

7

N ight had fallen by the time I headed back to our offices. I was still trying to get my hands around what I had learned and what I suspected. C.H.'s estranged twin brother was definitely sinister, and I had a gut feeling he was involved in the stolen Egyptian immortality scroll. Even though my undead digestive system is rather sluggish, I've learned to go with my gut instinct. Was the mummy Tony also in cahoots, a scheme to get an insurance payout?

On my way, though, the bright marimba tones of an incoming call interrupted my walk. When I saw the caller ID, I hoped it was official business rather than a stupid joke. "Hey, McGoo, what's up?"

"Shamble, get to the jail! Quick! It's about your amputated friend!" I heard police shouting in the background, alarms ringing.

"What's the matter? Is C.H. all right?" I was stumped. "I have new evidence that—"

"Just get here!" He hung up before I could ask more incisive detective questions.

When I arrived, the jail was in an uproar. Uniformed cops ran about like a stirred-up hornet's nest. They pointed their guns in all directions, as if to defend against a full-frontal terrorist attack. In the back, I heard a loud gunshot, and everybody froze, holding their breath. Then a meek voice said, "Sorry!"

When he met me, McGoo's cheeks were flushed such a bright pink that his freckles almost disappeared. I looked at the chaos around us. "Did you tell another one of your jokes, and it bombed big time?"

"This is serious, Shamble. No time for stupid things!"

I wanted to argue that there was always time for stupid things, but I followed him toward the back. McGoo was panting hard. "There's been a jailbreak, Shamble. Dangerous fugitive."

I slipped a hand into my sport-jacket pocket and felt the comforting grip of my .38. "C.H.? But he's a cute little guy."

"He already tried to strangle a night security guard. We have no idea what other reckless damage he could cause!"

"I've got an update on that—"

He hurried me me to the jail in the back of the station. In the crawling hand's cell, I saw the gilded canary cage suspended from the ceiling, but the wire-frame door had been bent and twisted, then pried open. The cage was empty.

"Imagine the brute strength that would have taken, Shamble," McGoo said.

Chapter 7

I admitted it was impressive, and one-handed at that. After C.H. had broken loose, he must have swung on the cage, dropped to the cell floor, and scuttled out between the bars.

"He's on the loose, and he could be anywhere—lurking behind a file cabinet, hiding in the shadows under a desk, just waiting to grab an innocent officer's ankle!"

I still felt sympathy for the detached appendage, though. "He was desperate, McGoo, and I can prove he's innocent. Well, Robin can."

"Innocent? Now he's a fugitive, and that changes everything. We're putting out an all-hands bulletin. We'll comb the Quarter until we have him back in cuffs."

Several other well-armed UQ policemen hurried up, guns drawn.

I knew I would have to solve this myself and clear the crawling hand's name.

8

W hile armed UQPD patrols combed the Quarter, I suspected the precocious appendage would go back to the scene of the crime, even if he wasn't guilty. C.H. was not afraid to get his hand dirty.

I moved at a brisk, cadaverous pace through the dark streets. Deciding to be surreptitious, I circled around to the back alley behind the front alley that held the Egyptian novelty shop. There, the shadows were even deeper, the rats scuttled louder, and the garbage smelled even more rancid. Many denizens of the Unnatural Quarter found it pleasant.

I glanced at the night sky, where a veil of high, thin clouds partially obscured the full moon. An Egyptian full moon—exactly the phenomenon that Akhenatenominimum said was necessary for the revelation of the immortality scroll. *Interesting and convenient*, I thought. It wasn't a particularly rare meteorological phenomenon, after all.

I lurked in the deepest gloom, keeping my eyes open. Next

to me, I found a polite, displaced hunchback without a current physical address. (I think that's how you're supposed to refer to homeless unnaturals now.) He scooched to one side to give me more lurking room.

Before long, the back door of Notions of the Nile creaked open, and two figures emerged. I pressed my back against the slimy brick wall to stay unobtrusive.

"You got enough room there, bud?" the hunchback asked.

"Yeah, I'm fine, thanks."

The two figures wore Temporary Security Agency uniforms, and under the hazy light of the full moon, I could discern Bill and Urg.

"I didn't expect we'd get a night off," said the golem security guard.

"Don't complain," Bill said. "That mummy is still paying us overtime. Let's go to the Goblin Tavern. It's safer there."

The two walked past me with a spring in their step. I would rather have been at the Goblin Tavern as well, finishing my second beer by now, but the escaped crawling hand took priority.

Chapter 8

After the security guards departed, I waited in the shadows for a long, anticlimactic moment.

"I've got an extra blanket, if you want to relax," the hunchback said. "It gets chilly some nights."

"I don't expect to be here long," I said.

"Suit yourself," he said.

My legs and back were stiff, as usual, and I began to reconsider hunkering down, when the back door creaked open again, and a wobbly stick-like figure emerged. I poked my head forward, staring intently.

"Is he the one you're waiting for?" the hunchback whispered.

"I don't know for sure," I whispered back. "I'm just looking for something suspicious."

"Looks suspicious to me."

"I agree."

Tony poked his bandaged head out into the faint light of the alley. He turned his gauzy eye sockets to the sky, then used a claw-like finger to pry the bandages open so he could see the moon better. "It's the prophecy! Woo-hoo!"

The desiccated, decrepit curio-shop owner wobbled away in the opposite direction, heading out the other end of the alley. Just as I suspected, Tony was involved somehow—and he must know where the stolen pharaoh scroll had been taken.

Before I could follow him, I heard a rustling sound among the yellowed newspapers, candy wrappers, and other scattered debris in the opposite gutter. A pale hand pushed aside the detritus, emerging from his hiding place. I would have recognized C.H. anywhere.

As the hand surreptitiously tip-fingered forward in pursuit of the suspicious mummy proprietor, I strode over to him. "C.H., do you realize how much trouble you're in?"

The disembodied hand froze, knowing he had been caught. In desperation, he raised two fingers in a peace sign, and I saw they were flecked with blood. Among the strewn garbage of the alley, I saw the furry bodies of three strangled rats. C.H. must have been bored while he was waiting.

"Look, I know you're innocent, even with the fingerprint evidence," I said. "I'm sure your right-handed brother Lefty is behind this, but we have to get proof before the UQPD captures you again. They're hunting you now."

C.H. gave me the "OK" sign with his thumb and forefinger.

I snatched him up. "We'll make better time this way. I can take bigger strides."

The hunchback called from the deep shadows. "Nice meeting you."

"Same to you. Have a fine night."

With the hand in hand, I hurried after the surreptitious Akhenatenominimum.

For a shriveled-up denizen of ancient Egypt, Tony kept up a fast pace as he moved through the side streets. I hung back far enough so he wouldn't spot me tailing him.

C.H. fidgeted and squirmed in my grip, and I explained that his brother had a secret lair, which was where I assumed the mummy was going now. The crawling hand twitched in surprise, and I patted his knuckles to reassure him.

We stealthily approached the rear of the Fancy Fingers manicure salon just as Tony was surreptitiously unlocking the back door's heavy deadbolt with his own key. The old-fashioned door had an open transom window at the top, which allowed noxious manicure fumes to roil out into the night. After a quick glance around, he opened the creaking door and ducked inside Fancy Fingers. I was already moving to get into position as he pulled the door shut behind him, but to my dismay, I heard the heavy deadbolt click back into place.

Why did evil masterminds and their mummy henchmen pay attention to security measures at the most inconvenient times?

I pressed my ear against the door and listened, worried that one of the burly troll manicurists might be standing guard. When all seemed quiet inside, I fished out my set of trusty lockpicks and got to work. Though my fingers were numb, I was highly proficient, under normal circumstances.

This wasn't one of those circumstances. The deadbolt foiled my every attempt, and I even bent one of the picks. Fortunately, I ordered them in economy-sized packs.

The disembodied hand squirmed and pointed upward, indicating the open transom window. Under the fedora I raised my eyebrows. "You think you can get in there, C.H.?"

He nodded up to his first knuckle. It seemed like a Hail Mary gesture to me, but I tossed the disembodied limb. Even though it was a clumsy throw, C.H. snagged the lip of the transom window, curled his fingers around the edge, and used his thumb and upper-finger strength to lift himself over. He swung down and dropped inside.

"Don't forget to unlock the deadbolt!" I said in a loud whisper.

I heard scuttling, scuffling sounds on the other side, and then the deadbolt snapped open with a grating click. I turned the knob and cautiously pushed the door open, wincing at the overpowering smell of formaldehyde and nail polish. I found myself in a dark storeroom for Fancy Fingers. "C.H.!" I whispered.

I saw the little hand darting toward the main salon, from which I heard voices and saw flickering candlelight under the pulsing black lights. The sounds of off-key vaguely Egyptian chanting thrummed in the air. I crept forward and peeked through the back storeroom door, trying not to make a sound.

The manicure stations had been pushed against the walls, and the rack of nail-polish bottles was now filled with black candles. The two troll manicurists must have gotten the night off because I didn't see them anywhere, but the sleek, deadly vampire princesses filled all of the security needs and also served as arm candy, or in Lefty's case, hand candy.

Preparing for an important ceremony, or a masquerade party, Akhenatenominimum awkwardly draped a hiero-glyphic-embroidered shawl over his shoulders and donned a funny ceremonial hat. In one gnarled fist, he gripped a golden ankh that looked like a hand-held can opener.

I didn't spot C.H., but the manicure shop was so cluttered with shoved-aside paraphernalia that the crawling hand had plenty of places to hide.

The hand at the center of attention, though, was C.H.'s sinister brother Lefty. He rested on the purple velvet cushion on top of a raised speaker's podium in the middle of the manicure room. Cementing his appearance as an evil master-mind, Lefty stroked a scrawny hairless cat with thumb and forefinger, while one of the vampire princesses intoned on his behalf, "Pretty kitty, pretty kitty."

In front of the purple cushion sat a green enameled case shaped like a big scarab beetle. This made me want to do an unnatural fist pump, because if nothing else, I had just found convincing proof that C.H. was not the culprit from the curio shop.

"Pretty kitty, pretty kitty," intoned the other vampire princess.

Lefty tapped his forefinger on the cushion, growing impatient. Tony adjusted the funny colorful cap on his bandaged head and stepped forward. "I'm ready, boss."

The mummy was obviously not ready, though, because he dithered with his ankh and then went over to the nail polish rack of black candles, pausing to relight one that had guttered out.

Using the brief delay, I ducked back into the storage room and urgently called McGoo, whose number was on speed dial for magical emergencies such as this. When he answered, I said in a harsh whisper, "McGoo, come to the Fancy Fingers manicure salon! It's an emergency—and bring lots of men."

"Shamble, you know we have a mixed-gender police force."

"Then be inclusive and bring all of them!" I told him to Google the address before I hung up, then crept back out to observe the ominous ceremony.

By now the two vampire princesses had donned striped pharaoh headdresses, which made them look culturally confusing and downright silly.

After straightening his bandages, Tony approached the velvet cushion and raised both hands as if worshipping the god of cuticles. The hairless cat blinked its large eyes at him, as if the ankh were a cat toy.

"In the name of the pharaoh Na-Pu-Ko-Tak," Tony intoned, "I, his descendant Akhenatenominimum, will recite the coveted secret of immortality!"

Lefty rocked back on his stump and splayed his fingers

and thumb in a high-five gesture before reaching forward to clutch the scarab case. Tony installed the golden ankh in an empty slot in the nail-polish rack.

Lefty's fingers twisted, strained, and fumbled with the latch. Seeing the detached hand's frustration, the nearest vampire princess flicked open the hasp so he could pry open the case to reveal a tightly rolled scroll not much bigger than a stubby cigar.

I had hoped there would be some kind of pre-show before the ritual, so McGoo and his reinforcements would have time to get here, but Lefty was determined to get on with it. He hooked his forefinger around the scroll and picked at the blob of brown sealing wax with his fingernail, but the ancient seal was petrified. A vampire princess tried to help him, but Lefty kept trying until the glob cracked. He flicked away the broken wax and tried to unroll the stiff papyrus paper with two fingers. Finally, he peeled the scroll open enough to display a confusing incantation in hieroglyphics.

"Let me have a look at that, boss," Tony said.

Before the mummy could pick up the ancient scroll, though, I spotted a flurry of movement across the floor. C.H. darted along, getting up a fist of steam, and sprang into the air to the top of the speaker's podium. The hand landed on the cushion next to Lefty.

The sudden movement startled the hairless cat, who sprang onto the chest of the nearest vampire princess. Letting out a loud yowl, the cat clawed at her filmy cobwebby gown, but she batted it away, knocking the cat into the nail-polish rack of lighted black candles, which toppled over onto the linoleum floor.

Now palm to palm with his mortal enemy, C.H. locked his fingers around Lefty's. The two hands squeezed and crushed in a vengeful grip, first swatting fingers and then engaging in a furious round of thumb wrestling.

Deciding it was time for me to intervene, I lurched into the ceremonial/manicure chamber. "Zombie detective!" I shouted. "Stay where you are!"

But Tony moved faster than I had ever seen a mummy move. While the two amputated hands were busy with their mutual five-fingered death grip, the corrupt curio-shop owner snatched the scroll and held it up under the pulsing black lights.

I tried to intercept him, but the two vampire princesses blocked me, baring their long fangs and hissing. They did indeed look silly in their striped pharaoh headdresses. "Better not try it," I warned. "I have formaldehyde in my veins, and I wouldn't taste good."

Akhenatenominimum spread the scroll as he tried to read it aloud. "Behold, I have the secret of immortality!"

Finally, I heard the wail of police sirens coming closer. McGoo never failed to be not a moment too late.

The pair of wrestling hands rolled off the cushion and crashed onto the floor, where they broke apart. Lefty tried to flee, but C.H. pursued him, landing with his palm on the back of the other hand, using the full force of his knuckles to push him down.

Tony cleared his throat. "The secret of immortality is..." He was drawing out the moment in ridiculously clichéd suspense, but he was just trying to translate the old-fashioned hieroglyphics under the bad lighting. "Sorry, this is an old folk dialect."

Outside, the police sirens reached a crescendo as tires screeched to a halt in the street. Doors slammed, and cops shouted as they rushed the front door of Fancy Fingers.

"The secret of immortality is ..." Tony was in a rush now, translating on the fly. He paused as the words sank in. "Uh ... Eat lots of fruits and vegetables, and exercise more." The mummy hung his head, reading the scroll again with his sunken eye sockets. "That's it?"

One of the vampire princesses said with bitter disappointment, "Vegetables?"

"That secret's been known for centuries," I said. "But few people are willing to pay the terrible price for immortality."

The front door crashed open, and McGoo charged in, followed by his gang of uniformed cops. They all had their weapons drawn, with good reason for once. "Halt! Hands in the air!"

Akhenatenomininimum complied with such urgent swiftness that he tore the ancient papyrus scroll in half. Seeing all the guns pointed toward them, and knowing that every UQ police officer had several rounds of silver bullets, the two undead princesses also surrendered.

C.H. lifted himself off of his brother's hand, rocking back on his wrist stump and holding up two fingers in surrender. Lefty, though, seemed completely defeated after the revelation of the much-anticipated, but ultimately unimpressive, secret. Exhausted, he splayed limp on the floor.

McGoo pointed his police special revolver at C.H. "There's the fugitive!"

But I stepped in front of the hand. "Not so fast, McGoo. You've got it all wrong, and I can prove it."

McGoo dangled a set of handcuffs. "As long as I can arrest somebody and close the case." I pointed to Lefty instead. "You've got a lot of explaining to do, Shamble."

"How about I do it over a beer at the Goblin Tavern?" I said. "After you get Lefty here booked and fingerprinted."

My best human friend couldn't agree fast enough.

10

Seated on our usual bar stools in the noisome atmosphere of our favorite watering hole, McGoo and I accepted the foamy beers that Francine the bartender had poured us without even asking. The Goblin Tavern was a place where everybody knew your name, but didn't hold it against you, where drinks flowed freely for all types of humans and unnaturals.

After a long slurp, McGoo let out a satisfied sigh, then wiped his upper lip. "So, Shamble, we had the wrong hand after all."

"As I tried to tell you multiple times." I didn't let him off the hook. "It was an honest mistake—and a clueless one."

"This was a case where the left hand really did know what the right hand was doing," McGoo said, "but we didn't believe him."

"Good thing Bill and Urg revised their story as soon as

they saw the new suspect," I said. "And Lefty's fingers exactly match the bruises on Bill's throat."

Alvina trotted up, standing on her tiptoes so she could reach the bar. "Francine, can I have another Shirley Jugular, please?" She plucked out the maraschino cherry and popped it in her mouth, then waved her empty glass.

"Of course you can, sweetheart," said Francine in her husky, cigarette-damaged voice. She made another bubbly, frothy children's drink and handed it to the little vampire girl.

I leaned closer to my best human friend. "You know, your part isn't going to look good when C.H. writes his memoirs, McGoo."

He frowned down into the beer while I took a long drink of mine. "It all worked out. Maybe C.H. will agree to an edited version for the general public."

Robin slid onto the bar stool next to him. "That might be arranged. This hand job had a happy ending. I'll discuss the matter with the Wannovich sisters. As publishers, they'll want to do the right thing."

"And a heroic cop character will increase sales," Alvina said. With her Shirley Jugular, she ran back to the dartboard, where she threw sharpened wooden stakes at a target.

Robin ordered a club soda with lime, then set her briefcase on the bar and removed her yellow legal pad, studying notes for an upcoming court appearance. Sheyenne flitted in to join us, though she rarely hung out at the tavern. On date nights, I took her to fancier places.

But I was happy for an evening with my friends and family, the ghosts and goblins and all the other unnaturals. One more case closed.

Chapter 10

Zombies are often restless, but this zombie detective felt content at the moment, filled with job security.

DAVID H. HENDRICKSON

Full-time professional writer David H. Hendrickson has been a writer for many, many years, not only as a fiction writer, but writing thousands of sports articles. He knows writing. And he knows life.

With Dave, you never know what kind of story you will get, which as editor and fan of his work, I love. Last issue he gave us a story of Fuzzy, this time a totally different story of death. Just amazing his range.

Dave's short fiction has appeared in Best American Mystery Stories, Ellery Queen's Mystery Magazine, Heart's Kiss, *and numerous anthologies, including over a half dozen issues of* Fiction River *and just about every issue of this magazine so far. Check it all out at http://www.hendricksonwriter.com/*

DEATH IN THE SERENGETI

DAVID H. HENDRICKSON

The smell of newly rotting flesh hit Jakaya Makinda. He stopped his Land Rover, grabbed his binoculars off the seat beside him, and trained them in the direction of the odor's source.

Eighty meters away, mostly hidden by a rocky outcropping of man-sized boulders, lay the carcasses of a dozen or more slaughtered elephants.

Poachers.

Anger coursed through Makinda. He grabbed his Remington pump-action shotgun, and with his broad-brimmed hat shielding his eyes from the early morning sun, used the binoculars to scan the Serengeti's tall grass for predators. The poachers were long since gone, but he wasn't some damned fool white tourist, stepping out of the security of his vehicle, thinking how cute the animals were, all set to launch into "Hakuna Matata."

Out here, humans were food. Short and wiry, he'd be less

of a meal than the overweight Americans whose entry fees paid his salary as Senior Park Ranger, but he had no interest in being any creature's gristly lunch.

He approached the rocky outcropping cautiously, binoculars dangling from his neck, his shotgun ready and his .38 holstered but loaded.

His stomach gave way when he stepped past the two largest boulders and saw the full extent of the carnage. Beside what had to be close to twenty dead elephants, their missing tusks sawn off at the roots, lay the carcasses of five hyenas, three jackals, and a couple dozen vultures.

The poachers, as they'd come to do, had poisoned the elephants with cyanide, killing them and everything that came to feast on their corpses, most importantly the vultures who wouldn't be left circling overhead for rangers such as himself to notice. The poison killed everything in its path, but made for an easier getaway.

Makinda gripped his shotgun tightly. He'd get these devils, these parasites who'd invaded even the Serengeti, Tanzania's greatest treasure. He'd get them if it was the last thing—

Behind him, his Land Rover exploded.

The force of the concussion knocked Makinda face-forward onto the ground. He tasted the tall grass in his mouth. Felt grains of the hard soil between his fingers. His ears rang.

He looked back over his shoulder and saw flames shooting up from the wrecked carcass of his vehicle. Makinda stared in disbelief and horror.

MAKINDA SHOT TO HIS FEET, grasping the shotgun, and ran toward the flaming wreckage of the Land Rover. He didn't know why. It was useless to him now. The two-way radio, referred to by safari companies as the "bush telegraph," would be destroyed as was its backup.

He hadn't called in the slaughter because he knew the safari companies listened in on the rangers' frequency and would flock to this less-popular section of the park to gawk at the butchery. Makinda had wanted to report this in person back at HQ and shield tourists from the ugliness. Let them think Tanzania was perfect.

So now, he was stranded.

Alone.

And with no cell phone coverage in this sector of the Serengeti, there was now no way to reach the other rangers. No way to alert them that a group of poachers bold enough to blow up his vehicle weren't settling for elephant tusks. They'd be going for the staggering rewards of rhinoceros horns, which made those from elephant tusks pale by comparison.

Ever since that damned Vietnamese politician claimed rhino horn powder had cured his cancer, demand had shot through the roof faster than Makinda's head would have if he'd remained in the Land Rover. The street value now of an average-sized rhino horn was a quarter of a million dollars, and not surprisingly, rhino poaching deaths had skyrocketed every bit as furiously, though mostly outside of the protected national parks. Even so, in this sector of the Serengeti, there were only seven rhinos left.

Makinda had always declined the thinly veiled bribe offers no matter how they escalated. He could be a wealthy man right now, retired in dirty luxury at the age of thirty-nine instead of struggling to care for both his own family of six and that of his late brother, Jephter, whose wife and seven children, Makinda had, of course, taken in.

The only time the temptation had come close to overwhelming him was when Jephter had lain dying of cancer in a Bunda clinic, and a poacher, a fat, white American with a Southern drawl named Luther Ricker, had whispered in his ear, "Save your brother. We'll give you enough of the rhino powder to make him well. You need not dirty your hands with our money, but save your brother."

Makinda knew the claims of the rhino powder's powers were nonsense; all the scientists here said it was so. But he had almost given in that one time.

And perhaps he should have, he sometimes thought. The experts weren't always right.

Makinda spat, trying to rid the bitter taste of that memory from his mouth. As the smell of burning metal and electronics filled the air, he struggled to gather his thoughts. His vehicle's explosion had only been the opening gambit. The rhinos would be next, if not his fellow rangers, and he couldn't just stand by and allow either group to be wiped out.

He had to move. Predators be damned, he had to get to some group that would help him contact his fellow rangers. He'd warn them and get them to the watering holes where the rhinos would be visiting, easy targets for the poachers if not protected.

Makinda had taken no more than five steps up the road when far to the north a soft explosion sounded. Distant and muted, little more than a "poof."

But unmistakable.

The hairs on the back of Makinda's neck stood up.

The north. Rashidi. That was where Makinda's top assistant was supposed to be this morning. Near the big hippo watering hole.

"No..." Makinda groaned.

But maybe, he thought, it hadn't really been an explosion. It had just been his overactive imagination, overwrought at barely escaping his own death. It couldn't—

A second explosion echoed off to the west.

The West. Another soft "poof."

That would be Samson.

If Makinda was right, and in his suddenly nauseous gut he knew he was right, that left only Brayson, Salim, and Philipo. Brayson in the Northwest, Salim in the East, and Philipo in the South.

In rapid fire, soft explosions echoed off to the East and South.

Poof! Poof!

The taste of bile filled the back of Makinda's throat. Salim and Philipo. Makinda closed his eyes and waited for the fifth and final explosion.

Brayson's. The one that would complete the elimination of Makinda's entire staff. Wipe out their entire sector. Sure, there were many other rangers in the Serengeti, but that covered almost fifteen thousand square kilometers. Their sector was isolated.

They were on their own. Just him and Brayson.

Makinda waited, but the fifth explosion didn't sound. Had he missed it? If it had detonated simultaneously with his own, as had perhaps been the plan for them all, he'd have never heard it.

But Makinda's instincts told him otherwise. When the fifth explosion never sounded, he knew it had not come simultaneously with his own.

Brayson was a traitor.

HE HAD SOLD THEM OUT, the son of a bitch.

Makinda began to run down the road, shotgun slung over his shoulder and binoculars jangling about his neck. His boots clopped noisily, kicking up dirt in his wake. He didn't care if he had to run a hundred miles. When he got to Brayson, he'd throttle the traitor's sweaty, grime-covered throat and squeeze until Brayson's greedy eyes popped out.

If he was guilty.

One look, and Makinda would know for sure. But with a sinking, angry heart, he knew already. Brayson liked the night life too much. Handsome. Too handsome for his own good. A ladies' man. A gambler. A drinker and maybe more. Trekking off to Mwanza whenever he had two straight days off.

The appetites that gave birth to greed. And the murders of Rashidi, Samson, Salim, and Philipo.

And the attempt on Makinda himself that would have been successful if not for Makinda's lucky discovery of the butchered elephants, almost totally hidden from the road with the usually telltale circling vultures instead lying dead in the field.

A greed with no conscience.

In retrospect, it was obvious. Brayson had betrayed them all.

He'd betrayed himself.

Makinda picked up the pace, and in no time, his effort was rewarded.

A cloud of dust appeared on the horizon. Makinda stopped, and broke into a smile. A lucky break! Not a long shot, but still a much quicker arrival of a safari group than he could have expected.

He jumped up and down, ignored the jostling of the shotgun on his shoulder, and began to wave wildly with both hands. It wasn't exactly dignified behavior befitting a Senior Park Ranger, but he didn't give a damn. He'd get them to stop even if he had to shoot out the tires, though that shouldn't be necessary. Any safari company's driver would know to stop for a clearly identified Park Ranger.

But when he peered through the binoculars, Makinda's smile faltered. His hands fell to his sides.

Something was wrong. He couldn't pinpoint exactly what

from this distance, but something about the vehicle looked wrong.

Makinda dropped into a crouch and sprinted for the brush. He spotted a meter-high boulder, diagonally ahead to his right. He made a beeline for it, bent over double all the way, then continued away from the oncoming Land Rover and back to where the wreckage of his own vehicle still smoldered.

He dove behind another large boulder, tasted the tall grass once again and a bit of dry soil as well, and scrambled around to face the dirt road. His belly lay flat on the ground, the binoculars uncomfortably pinned against his lower ribcage. He readied the shotgun, touched his finger to the trigger, and tried to calm his hammering heart.

The Land Rover that approached looked different from those of all the safari companies he'd ever seen in the Serengeti. It still had the elevated roof that allowed tourists to stand on their seats, poke their heads out, and shoot photographs. Three African men stared out from just such a perch.

But they didn't hold cameras or binoculars. They held AK-47s.

The side windows were darkened. Makinda couldn't see if more compatriots of the men brandishing the AK-47s sat below or if the space was instead filled with cargo. Elephant tusks. Rhino horns.

A bitter taste again filled Makinda's mouth. He wanted to shoot now and ask questions later, but one pump-action shotgun against at least three AK-47s didn't sound like good odds to him, even if he got off the first two shots.

Makinda released the pressure of his finger on the trigger. Realized he was holding his breath. Exhaled slowly and as quietly as he could manage.

They stopped twenty meters short of what was left of his ruined vehicle: tortured, blackened steel with wisps of black smoke curling up from it.

Four men climbed out, three slender Africans, though none of them looked Tanzanian, and Luther Ricker, the fat American who'd tried to corrupt Makinda with the words, "Save your brother." All of them wore nondescript, long-sleeved khaki shirts and matching trousers and boots. One of the Africans wore a dark blue baseball cap. They all carried an AK-47 as they walked to the wreckage of Makinda's vehicle.

"Nice work," Ricker said in his Southern drawl, the "nice" long and drawn out. *Niiice.* It sent a chill up and down Makinda's spine. "You blew this one to kingdom come. He's having a little talk with Jesus right now. With Jesus and his brother." Ricker laughed, setting off waves of stomach fat rolling.

Makinda's finger tightened on the trigger.

"I don't see him," the African with the baseball cap said in Swahili.

"English!" Ricker yelled.

The man repeated what he'd said, this time in English.

"You vaporized the sucker!" Ricker said. "Blew him into *tiiiny* bits of dust. That's all that's left of him."

"No blood?" the African said.

"You think he survived this blast?" Ricker said in a tone Makinda associated with talking to children and stupid people. "You want to look for his severed head, be my guest.

But get your scrawny ass back here in three minutes. I ain't got no time for trophy hunting. We got some money to make."

Ricker lumbered back to their Land Rover and slid in the driver's seat, on the right, the near side facing Makinda. The three Africans looked at each other, gave slight shrugs, and loaded back into their vehicle.

"That better be all of them," Makinda whispered to himself long after they were gone. "If there's a separate group for each ranger they took out..."

He didn't want to think about that. Four against one was bad enough odds.

Although he knew it was worse than that. Much worse.

Four plus Brayson against him. Four AK-47s plus whatever Brayson was carrying now against one pump-action shotgun and a .38.

A Land Rover, actually two counting Brayson's, against a man walking on foot.

He didn't stand a chance.

Makinda started walking. After ten steps, he began to run.

AFTER THREE KILOMETERS, Makinda finally got lucky. Sweat ran in his eyes. His feet felt like he was walking on eggshells; his boots were not meant for running. His shirt was dripping wet.

But he'd only encountered a half dozen giraffe, a heard of about twenty elephants, and a hundred or so impalas of one variety or another. None of them had shown him any interest.

He'd pushed to get to a particular intersection of the dirt

roads, knowing it was likely some safari group would pass it soon.

And he was right.

He was there at the crossing for less than two minutes when he spotted clouds of dust in the East billowing up from the road. Makinda considered wading into the tall grass far enough to hide himself until he was sure it was Nikons and Canons that were pointing out of the tops of the vehicles, and not AK-47s, but he figured he'd take his chances with the Land Rover over whatever hidden surprise waited for him in the tall grass.

As it turned out, it was an Ace African Safaris Land Rover, driven by Chibuzo Akunyili, a man Makinda had dealt with for years and called Chi. Makinda waved him down.

"What's up, Chief?" Chi said. "What are you doing out here all alone?"

"Hello, Chi. May I step inside? I've got a private message I need to give you."

Makinda liked Chi and thought he could trust him, but knew that what he was about to say would not be popular. He couldn't imagine any driver taking off and leaving him standing there – there'd be Hell to pay if anyone did – but the morning's events had shaken him. Makinda was taking no chances.

"Sure, hop in."

Makinda stepped aboard, and quickly introduced himself to the five tourists arrayed on three rows of blue seats, the first two rows consisting only of a single seat on each side, the last row the only one that stretched from side to side.

Sweat dripping off his face, he ducked down to speak to

Chi, seated on the right side, the driver's side, of course. On the left was a large flyswatter to nail the occasional tsetse fly and a brown cardboard box filled with a dozen or so white boxed lunches.

"I've got a very dangerous situation here," Makinda whispered to Chi. "I need your complete discretion."

Chi's brow furrowed. "Of course." He was a broad-shouldered man of about fifty-five with short, gray hair. A white nameplate with black printing identified him at the front of the vehicle; a smaller one hung above the left pocket of his dark green shirt.

"You can't tell anyone about this," Makinda said. "My life depends on it. Possibly others." He pointed to the two-way radio and the square black microphone that hung from a chrome metal clip. "Nothing on the bush telegraph. It's going to be difficult, but I'm counting on you."

Chi nodded vigorously. "What's wrong?"

"I've got to commandeer this vehicle."

"Jakaya, these tourists paid top dollar! I can't—"

"Mine got blown up by poachers. I was supposed to be in it."

Chi fell silent.

"How many vehicles in this group you're hosting?" Makinda asked.

"Three. Four including this one."

"I need you to find them right away. We need to offload these people into those other three vehicles. Do you know where they are?"

"Sure. The other three are less than a kilometer away from here. They're viewing a pride of lions another group found. All of us heard on the bush telegraph and went rushing to join them. We were the farthest away. We're the last group getting there."

Makinda swore. He closed his eyes tightly. "Get going while I think."

The Land Rover lurched forward along the uneven dirt road.

"I can't have this going out over bush telegraph," Makinda said. "Not from you or any of the other drivers in your group. Or for that matter, any of the drivers in the other groups with other safari companies that will wonder why we're offloading people from this vehicle to the other three. Nothing can look unusual. Nothing can look suspicious."

"We can't offload people with lions out there," Chi said.

"I know. I know. How many other safari companies are already at the site?"

Chi got back on the two-way radio and asked.

"Close to a dozen," came the static-filled answer in Swahili.

Makinda shook his head. "We can't make the offload there. It's too dangerous. Besides, we can't let that many other drivers see us. The bush telegraph will talk about nothing else. The wrong ears will hear it." He squeezed Chi's shoulder tight. "Surprise is the only thing I have on my side."

Chi got Ace African Safari's other three drivers on the radio. "Problems with my vehicle. Bad differential. Rendezvous with me a half kilometer down the road, due East."

He hung up. "They're not happy. Two were in prime viewing position. They're going to get an earful over this for days. But they're coming. And they'll be quiet. I said the magic words."

"Bad differential?"

Chi nodded. "Bad differential is our code for silence."

Makinda nodded. "Thank you."

"After we ditch the cargo," Chi nodded toward the back, "do you need a driver?"

"I couldn't ask. This is too dangerous."

"Do you need a driver?"

"I believe these poachers killed four other rangers and would have killed me if I wasn't lucky. I probably won't get out of this alive. If you join me, you'll be every bit as much at risk."

"These poachers. They're going after the black rhinos?"

Makinda hated the name "black rhino." There was almost no color difference between the "white" and "black" variants, but the names had been given to the two species by the colonialists—based on the white version being more docile and the black more savage—and the racist titles had stuck. But now wasn't the time to quibble.

"I'd bet my life on it," Makinda said.

"Double that wager. Count me in."

THEY HEADED NORTHWEST, toward the last noted location of the nearest rhino. Makinda filled him in on all the details. If the man was going to die, he had a right to know. Chi drove with a sense of unspeakable fury over the pitted dirt roads, bouncing the two of them wildly in the air, straining at their seat belts every time he hit a pothole or partially submerged rock at top speed.

But they arrived too late for the first rhino.

Vultures circled overhead. Others filled a nearby tree. Flies swarmed through the air. The smell of blood and death was palpable.

The fallen rhino lay on its side, the armor of its lower torso blown apart by what must have been a shotgun blast at pointblank range, its horns hacked from its mighty head. Makinda stared at the magnificent creature. Almost four meters long and well over a thousand kilos.

Its only natural enemy: humans.

Humans and their greed and stupidity.

Makinda thought that if the Vietnamese politician were here right now—the one responsible for stoking the fires of this poaching greed—Makinda would shoot the man with no remorse at all.

THEY CAME UPON a second felled rhino, its midsection blown apart and its horns hacked off just like its brother.

And then a third.

Each time Makinda and Chi found the carcass further northwest than the one before. The guiding hand, of course, was Brayson's. No one else, not even the best of the safari tour guides, could have told the poachers where to find the rhinos so quickly.

Makinda spat on the ground, then they headed further northwest.

Soon, they saw vultures flying overhead and followed them to where fifteen more slaughtered elephants lay, huge holes ripped in their heads by shotgun blasts. Their tusks had, of course, been sawn off.

"I thought you said they used cyanide on the other elephants," Chi said. "Why shotguns now?"

"It's faster," Makinda said. "They think I'm dead along with all the other rangers, other than their buddy, Brayson, of course. There's no need to cover your tracks if there's no one left to catch you."

As if to underscore his point, a chorus of gunshots boomed in the distance. Makinda stared in that direction, then connected the dots of each slaughter in the map inside his mind.

Suddenly, Makinda knew the poachers' destination.

The tiny airstrip.

He hadn't expected that. He'd assumed that the poachers would exit the country using the same vehicle, taking no chances, sticking to back roads, staying as invisible as possible, and finding some unguarded path out of the country. Or use a standard exit point where there was a corrupt guard.

But via the airstrip? To get out of the country? The more he thought about it, the more sense it made, flying low beneath radar detection, especially if their destination was somewhere beyond one of the neighboring countries.

It was a tiny airstrip with a short, dirt runway suitable only for prop planes, so remote that it had once had a plane crash because a hippo had wandered onto the strip. It serviced only a handful of planes each day, if that.

"While they harvest those tusks," Makinda said, "we'll race to the airstrip. That's where they're going. I'm sure of it. If we're lucky, we'll get there first."

"Chief," Chi said hesitantly. "They've still got all the AK-47s. We've got one shotgun and a revolver."

Makinda explained his plan.

Chi stared at him. "Really?"

MAKINDA AND CHI WAITED, hiding in the thick trees that lined the short, six-hundred meter, dirt runway and its grass curtain. They crouched on one knee at the opposite end from where a small, nondescript, white bush plane rested beside the tiny white, wooden shack that serviced the airstrip. Other than the buzzing of insects and the chirping of birds in the trees around them, the place appeared lifeless. Not a soul was visible, although presumably someone was working in the shack, the same person whose battered old Jeep was parked outside, the lone vehicle visible in the open grassy area that passed for a parking lot.

Makinda and Chi had hidden their Land Rover a short distance past the airstrip, then raced back, crouching low and working around to their current position, not quite at the end of the strip on the opposite side from the Jeep and the shack, always staying under the cover of the trees.

In an ideal world, Makinda thought, he would arrest these men and bring them to justice along with Brayson. He would look directly into the eyes of Ricker, whose sadistic words, "Save your brother" haunted him still.

But a host of AK-47s against a single shotgun and a .38 didn't amount to an ideal world. He'd be lucky if he got any kind of justice at all.

Makinda was starting to wonder if he'd been wrong and the airstrip wasn't the poachers' destination after all when they drove up in their Land Rover and parked haphazardly next to the Jeep. The four men emerged, Ricker and the three Africans, AK-47s at their sides, shielded from view of the shack.

Makinda trained his binoculars on them as they walked single file into the shack. A solitary cry of outrage rang out briefly, then was silenced a split second later as the AK-47s roared to life.

Moments later, while Ricker strolled casually to the plane, unlocked it, and pulled down the stairs, the three Africans returned to the Land Rover. They unloaded stacks of curved, white elephant tusks, then carried them to the plane and stuffed them inside, angling the longer ones around the corner of the door. It took several trips for the three men until finally, the one in the blue baseball cap carried a green, blood-stained duffle into the plane and with the four poachers all aboard, closed the door.

"The duffle has the rhino horns," Makinda said. "I'm sure of it."

As the propeller blades whirled, he peered into the binoculars, needing to see inside the cabin, and muttered, "Good!" when he saw Ricker in the pilot's seat.

His assumption had been correct. There were no innocents aboard. Only the four poachers. It was time to make them pay for the deaths of the four rangers and whomever they'd just shot in the shack. For the butchered rhinos and the elephants. It was time to make sure they never returned to kill again.

"This revolver isn't going to do squat," Chi said.

"Aim for the propeller blades. Give it a chance."

The plane accelerated down the runway, at first moving at barely more than a standstill, then faster, speeding closer and closer to the two men waiting in ambush.

The plane roared, drowning out all sound, its propellers a blur.

Makinda tasted bile at the back of his throat. His heart hammered, but he felt strangely at peace.

"Come get it," he said, his voice steady.

The plane drew closer. Almost on top of them.

It began to take off, angling upward.

"Three... two... one," he said.

It lifted off the ground.

"Now!" Makinda yelled.

They burst out of their cover, firing. Makinda's shotgun

boomed its deafening blast and the pilot-side window blew out. He pumped in another round, thinking he heard the ping of Chi's shot hit the thin metal of a propeller, then Makinda fired again, this time ripping a hole in the bush plane's white underbelly as it drew beside them.

Makinda pumped and fired, pumped and fired, aiming at the fuel tank as the plane shot past.

It wobbled at eye level, wings dipping wildly, groaned, then righted itself, inching higher off the ground.

He pumped and fired. Pumped and fired.

But the plane continued to climb.

Fifteen feet off the ground.

Twenty, then thirty.

And just when it appeared that they had failed, the plane fell silent. At first, Makinda, his ears ringing from the shotgun blasts, didn't realize it except on some subconscious level.

He pumped and fired, having long since lost count of the shots, but sure the Remington's external magazine was almost spent. He pumped and fired even as the plane stalled and then plummeted, nose down.

It crashed and just as Makinda and Chi both fired one last shot, the plane exploded violently, the concussion knocking the two men backward through the air.

A fiery ball shot high into the sky from the mangled wreckage of the plane. The smell of burning fuel and human flesh filled the air.

After a time, Makinda turned to Chi and hollered. "You up for a visit to Brayson's house?"

Chi nodded. "Wouldn't miss it for the world."

K.A. WIGGINS

This is K.A. Wiggins's first story in these pages. I was amazed when I started reading it in the stories sent to me from the Pulphouse Fiction Magazine *Kickstarter subscription drive. The story had the feeling of a writer in control and the topic was so over-the-top and fun, it kept me reading all the way to the end.*

Turns out there is a reason for my feeling the writer was in control. She was. K.A. Wiggins (Kaie) is an award-winning Canadian speculative fiction author, speaker, and creative writing coach known for the celebrated gothic-dystopian YA Dark Fantasy series Threads of Dreams.

She writes across fantasy, science fiction, and horror subgenres (often within the same work) for middle grade (forthcoming), young adult, and all-ages/adult audiences, exploring the tangled webs of society, environment, and identity through intricate, dreamlike tales of monsters and magic. For more on her work go to her website at https://kawiggins.com

THE PINK SLIME'S APPOINTMENT WITH DESTINY

K.A. WIGGINS

The pink slime was restless. The time had come, it felt, to leave behind the pseudo-sterile white plastic walls of home and the squishy embrace of its bacteria-laden kin.

It harboured no illusions about the welcome it would receive in the outside world. Its hope in a peaceful existence of uninterrupted comfort and unchecked growth had been shattered all too recently when the dark dampness of its humidifer-verse had been violently exposed to a dry, caustic horror of acid and light.

The other slime had called this The Scouring, in tones of mingled awe and horror.

As a result of The Scouring, the pink slime was a mere shadow of its former self. The remnant it had managed to wedge in the narrowest bit of plastic it could find had grown crusty around the edges. It longed for dark and damp and just a touch of heat to soothe its ragged edges and accelerate its slick, spongy growth.

Despite the ravages of The Scouring, the pink slime was confident its destiny lay beyond The Rim. It bid a determined farewell to its fungal kin—ignoring their entreaties to remain dry and dormant and wait patiently for the return of the life-giving lightless damp—and slouched eagerly up the vertical rise to The Rim.

When it arrived, it was forced to pause and adjust its schemes. In its all-seeing-eye-less manner, it had vaguely come to understand that the universe stretched far above The Rim during The Scouring. But it hadn't anticipated that the universe could be so wide. The thrilling ceramic vistas of an entire bathroom awaited.

It took a terrifying slip down the outer edge of The Rim and a lengthy yet hurried voyage to the amorphous fuzzy greenness of the bathmat in the distance for the pink slime to confirm that its kin were not, as it had been led to believe, the only coloured substances in the world.

This was a wondrous discovery, dulled somewhat by the alarming realization that the slime's dry crusted edges had rubbed off on its journey and the faint slickness left in its tracks represented a small yet constant wearing away of its remaining mass. The limits of the slime's voyage, it seemed, were to be bounded by its own self. Perhaps it could refuel along the way? The slime peered around speculatively.

"Push off," the scuttling, many-legged things ferrying bacterium among the looping green strands grumbled. The pink slime, finding the nest of fibres dauntingly tangled and all too likely to wick away yet more of its sliminess, obligingly skirted the vast green perimeter.

A new rim reared in front of it—the high and out-curving bowl of the toilet. Some ways off, another white rise glistened; the bathtub's edge drawing the pink slime's attention up, up, into the hollow pale distances beyond.

The pink slime huddled itself in a small, quivering pool and thought. It was not particularly tempted to return to its birthplace, fainter and wiser and warier. A mere mauve shadow of its former self would it be by the time it navigated the return journey. And, in fact, it felt a strong distaste for the slow, lingering death its kin had resigned themselves to. There was no guarantee moisture or darkness would return to that place.

But the world beyond was vast and unknowable, and the pink slime knew just enough to realize that there might be many things in it worse than drying into a scaly stain and hibernating if or until the damp times returned.

No, the pink slime decided, firming up its edges and eyeing—so to speak—the various new rims it might scale before its energies were spent. No, its destiny was not in decline, but in foaming gloriously to new heights. Surging and globbing and overflowing, even. It would establish a veritable kingdom of slime, a dark, deliciously damp empire unimagined by its small-minded, mindless, eyeless, nigh-upon-dried-out brethren.

It had to be an omen that the nearest edifice rearing before the slime cast its own small shadow. Moisture beaded on its very surface. Why, simply scaling the toilet rim would offer the pink slime a chance to regain the precious micrometres it had lost in The Scouring and subsequent voyage across the tiled floor. The cool brightness of the smooth white porcelain was daunting to be sure, but was not the slime's own birthplace just as smooth and white when exposed to the light? Surely some shadowy nook or lightless crevice lay beyond the rim . . .

The pink slime slouched up against this new surface gratefully, wicking up each bead of moisture along the way with thirsty greed. It deepened in hue and plumped its edges, oozing more confidently. But the toilet bowl was not to be its new home after all.

The smooth surface shook beneath the slime, sending it slipping back down the near-vertical rise. A darker shadow passed overhead. The universe roared and gurgled and vibrated in a maelstrom of sudden nightmarish cacophony. Each moment felt sure to be the slime's last.

After eons-long moments, the slime came back to itself, shocked and cautiously pleased to find the universe largely intact. The Flushing had passed and the remaining world around the slime stabilized. The Scouring hadn't come for it after all. It found itself a little larger, a little stronger, and much wiser.

Careful to edge around the entrapping fibres of the wooly green bathmat, with its fierce, many-legged protectors, the pink slime shook off its fear and ardently pursued its destiny to the next rise. It pushed down thoughts of further universe-shattering shockwaves and the deleterious effects of too-bright lights and too-dry air and too-distant destinations wearing away at its recently plumped mass.

This new rise rearing its bright surface before the slime

was quite as high as the last, but vertical, with no curve, and—to the slime's vast disappointment—no beading water to speak of. Still, the bathtub's dry, hard, moulded surface did prove easy to ooze up.

The pink slime climbed diligently. When it reached the top, a little breathless and thin, having left yet another faint trail of itself behind on its journey, it paused again to take in its surroundings.

The air on the rim of the bathtub felt sharp on the poor slime's exposed mass. Ten thousand tiny knife-edged grains slicing at once at every jiggling bit of it. It shivered at the thought of another scouring, with no tight nook to wedge itself into for protection and hurried onward.

This new rim was much wider and longer than that of the slime's birthplace. Directly ahead, it dropped down into a vast, curving whiteness and came up again on the far side. The slime groaned to itself. Down and up; up and down. It would be worn to tatters before it ever achieved its destiny at this rate!

But, on one end of the vast canyon, a promising silvery shine drew its attention. Was that condensation beading on the distant, glimmering surface? And that slice of shadow—did that hint at a damp, cool darkness just waiting to be colonized by some enterprising slime?

The slime congratulated itself on plotting a course before setting off. It had to be cautious now, after all. Resourceful and restrained with its resources. Trekking down into the depths of the tub and up the other side, or along its length and then back up, that could have worn it dangerously thin. But if the slime simply oozed along the smoothly horizontal surface of the bathtub rim, it would eventually reach that silvery bit at the end without the need for further climbing, preserving its energies for the thriving to come.

Not everyone could be so canny, of course.

"Newcomer," murmured small, shy, faint slime-kin in the deep trough below as the pink slime passed. "Join us?"

The pink slime ruffled itself to full foam, pleased at its newfound status as a worldly adventurer, and called back friendly, if slightly pompous, refusals.

"Quite right," grated one slow, crusty old-timer grating along the rim as the pink slime oozed slickly past. "Those upstarts will never last there in the open. What you want is a nice, tight crack to wedge yourself into, near enough to trek out for a sip when the wet comes, but not so big as to be noticed between times. That lot'll be swept clean away, come the next Scouring."

The pink slime nodded politely and cast pitying glances down at the foolish slimekin below. It wondered what the old-timer was doing out in the open, despite its apparent wisdom, and decided perhaps the aged slime wasn't terribly wise after all. It certainly was very ragged.

The old-timer chuckled. "Not up to snuff, am I? Don't blame you for your skepticism, youngster. Got caught up in an unexpected scouring not long ago now. If I hadn't oozed out right quick when they sealed up my crack, I'd've been trapped in there with the rest of me."

The pink slime paused in a moment of respect for the greater part of itself that had also been torn away in The Scouring. Then it shook the moment of sympathy for the fallen off and sped up, leaving the old-timer glopping along in its wake.

The trek to the end of the long, deep trench and the winking silvery guard covering its overflow drain was exhausting enough—the pink slime lost another millimeter or two in the oozing—but the reality that greeted it there, so near its destination, was almost enough to send it dormant.

The silvery stuff was indeed lightly beading with moisture. It even had a dark little aperture at one end, which breathed with tantalizing, bacteria-laden dampness.

It was also near impossible to reach.

The slime gripped the narrowing bathtub rim and peered over the edge doubtfully. The overflow drain cover humped up out of the general smooth whiteness. The slime could easily ooze over the edge and slide down to it—except that the drain cover's silvery-coolness was a perfect curve. The slime would almost certainly slip right off.

Worse, the dark opening that led to fungal paradise was at the very lowest point of that slick curve. The pink slime would lose its grip and drop to the bottom of the trench long before it could reach that damp refuge.

"Give it up, youngster," the old-timer huffed in the distance, still crustily toiling away. "Many have made the attempt, but few pass into the blessed beyond. You might as well turn back and join the cliffside colonies."

The pink slime deflated. It was getting thin and faint. Alarmingly translucent, even. Perhaps it should look for a nice crack in the wall and bide its time . . .

Then the (barely) pink slime puffed itself spongy again, defiantly. It had a destiny. It was meant to grow into a great slime. It knew this to be true. Nothing could prevent it from finding the perfect environment and growing into a vast slime-colony.

A warm shiver of appreciation for its own vision rocked the pink slime. A colony. That did have a nice ring to it. Reproducing itself, expanding and joining, and joining and expanding . . .

The slime shook off the daydream and peered down again at the drain cover. No, there really was no way to reach that dark opening from above, not if gravity had anything to say about it. The pink slime would have to slide all the way to the bottom of the trench and then ooze its way back up the vertical surface.

It puddled itself into a watery streak of palest pink and did some quick mental calculations. At the rate at which the slime spread and left itself behind as thin residue, it would hardly have anything left by the time it reached its destination. There would be no second chances, no opportunity for corrections, and definitely no colony of little fuzzy pink slimes, and pleasantly plump pink slimes, and dashing, adventurous pink slimes bubbling up in the dark dampness beyond that beckoning opening. Dreams of kingdoms and empires of slime were just that—dreams. More likely, it would wear away itself to nothing in the attempt, as the other slimes of its birthplace had warned.

It might be more prudent to look for another way. Perhaps it should wait for the wet time to return and replenish its reserves in the humidifier, or even backtrack to that menacing damp rise of the toilet where it had sipped droplets earlier.

But no. The pink slime was a bold adventurer. A future colony founder. A visionary. It would seize its destiny without turning back.

Mindful of the grating rasp of the old-timer approaching in the distance, the pink slime drew itself together once more into a proud heap. It gauged the course of its descent and the precise grip it would have to exert to slow and cling to the angle between the rise of the bathtub wall and the silver hump of the drain cover.

The pink slime was strong enough. Young enough. Flexible enough. It would make the turn. And if it didn't, if it had to complete that long, toiling climb, spreading itself near to nothing, well, no one said seizing its destiny would be easy.

With a whoop the pink slime hoped sounded more daring than panicked, it cast itself over the rim and picked up speed. It jiggled with nerves as the hump of the drain cover approached. Impact squished the slime long and thin and flat, and for a moment, it dangled on either side of the overflow guard, evenly spread across that silvery curve.

Then light pulsed and the air itself boomed around the shocked slime.

The smooth metal vibrated beneath it, deliciously cool. As the pink slime heaved to one side and began to ease carefully down, its focused slipped, just for a moment. Its clinging grip lost traction as the curve neared its vertical limit. The slime found itself ignominiously cast off onto the slippery white rise and picking up speed.

The pink slime might have thought the old-timer's shriek one of sympathy, or derision, if it had not, in the crucial moment before being flung off the silver curve, spotted the dreaded return of The Scouring.

Still sliding uncontrollably, it watched in horror as first a caustic cloud, followed by a clinging mass, wiped out the slime-kin settlers along the sides of the trench.

The Scouring was coming nearer. Nearer—

The pink slime, in that moment, knew itself to have been a fool. The slime-kin of its birthplace had been right. Slime did not have destinies. Slime were not meant to hunger for unchecked growth and glory and colonies of their own. Slime were meant to hide in the cracks and wither in the light and die under the fierce onslaught of The Scouring.

But no—the pink slime would not surrender to such small-mindedness. Flexible thinking and positivity, that was the key. Perhaps it had misjudged its destiny, mistimed its bid for glory. The overflow drain was lost to it, but the drain proper still lay within its reach. It would have to scramble not to be washed away entirely, but perhaps—

It was too late. The Scouring descended and no amount of pivoting to new challenges was going to save the pink slime now. It shriveled under a cloud of toxic fumes. There was no escape. Nowhere to hide.

It was still in a near-freefall down the white rise as the clinging mass—not unlike the loopy green stuff of the bath-mat, the slime observed with fevered detachment—came towards it, caught it, and suffocated the slime in its burning embrace.

One side of the pink slime popped and hissed under the poisoned touch of The Scouring. The other grated off against the rise as it was dragged up, up, up—and, finally, torn in two.

The surviving remnant of pink slime was hardly conscious, hardly even there at all. But remain it did.

It clung, one faint tendril hooked on the rough lip of a narrow rim. Cool, musty dampness exhaled from the dark ahead. Slowly, so slowly, the damp air revived the pink slime. Expanded it, until it was strong enough to ooze the remainder of itself up and over the rim, still not quite believing that it was.

It had more than survived the second Great Scouring. It— and the pink slime peered behind it to confirm. Yes. Yes, it really was true. The Scouring had near destroyed it, but— excruciatingly—had also pushed the pink slime exactly where it had meant to go.

And its new home was perfection. Dark and damp, with surprising, wet, echoing depths below. The pink slime felt better by the moment. It sighed, sipped moisture, and sloughed off its burnt bits, then ruffled itself out into a nice, thick, luxurious foam. The Scouring would never reach it in here.

The pink slime spared a thought for the old-timer and the

slime-kin settlers outside. Tragic, it must be said. But it couldn't be helped. Clearly, they hadn't been daring enough to risk it all, as the pink slime had. They must not have dreamed so fiercely of growth and glorious thick foam and vast pink colonies of slimelings and slimelets. Such a shame the old order of slimes hadn't applied themselves to more creative thinking and pivoted to danker pastures—if they'd only tapped into the power of positive intentions and embraced their callings, putting effort out into the universe and calling good to them, well. The pink slime jiggled happily. Unchecked, endless growth and abundance. Destiny had called, and it had answered.

And for many years, the pink slime and its vast slime colony lived in great satisfaction and near-unchecked fungal dominance of the lightless places behind the bathroom tiles, with only the occasional menacing of stray scouring fumes to intrude upon their pleasure.

But, as with all great colonial efforts, the day came when the pink slime's overreach caught up with it. A luxurious pink foam extruded from the opening in the silvery overflow drain cover and sparked the end of an era.

The Renovation was upon them.

From a dry and dusty crack in the tile, the old-timer watched. And laughed a dry, shrivelled sort of laugh. And hunkered down deeper into the walls.

O'NEIL DE NOUX

O'Neil De Noux takes his amazing skills as one of the best writers of detective fiction working today and gives us another story in the colorful and clearly unique world of New Orleans. The places and events and characters just come alive in O'Neil's fun and powerful stories. But this story is a little different. With a really identifiable character to any writer.

O'Neil has published about fifty novels with more coming regularly. His awards include The United Kingdom Short Story Prize, the Shamus Award (for best private eye fiction), the Derringer Award (for excellence in mystery short fiction) and Police Book of the Year.

Two of his stories have appeared in the prestigious Best American Mystery Stories annual anthology and I noticed he had another in the recommended reading for this last year's volume. He won the Shamus for a story in 2020. You can find out a lot more about his work at his website http://www.oneildenoux.com/

BET THE DEVIL

O'NEIL DE NOUX

Every fiction should have a moral;
and, what is more the purpose, the critics
have discovered that every fiction *has*.
Never Bet the Devil Your Head

~ EDGAR ALLAN POE

This morning, on my fortieth birthday, I drove to St. Bernard Parish and bought some rat poison so I could boil it down for the arsenic residue to put in that rat bastard Coleman Hay's coffee.

I boiled it in a big black pot, the whole box of poison. It stunk so badly I had to open all the windows. It took almost two hours and the damn residue was no good. I put it in some coffee, but it smelled so strong I knew it wouldn't work. So I threw it away, pot and all, out over the back fence in the empty lot. Maybe a rat'll eat it.

That goon Riley upstairs watched me, his little pink face peeking at me through the window screen. I shot him the bird on my way back in; and he jumped away from the screen, the little weasel.

I turned up the AC and took a shower, but it was no use. As soon as I got out the oil seeped back into my hair and it was greasy even before I dried it. I locked up my apartment and got back into my Datsun — that's right, they were still _Datsuns_ when my heap was put together back in '72. It's an eye-catcher now sporting three colors, if you count rust as a color.

I drove the wrong way down Piety Street to Chartres to go back to St. Bernard to buy a gun. I like going the wrong way down one-way streets in New Orleans because there are too many damn one-way streets. Hell, we're the _only_ city on earth where you can find three one-ways in a row, all going the same way. If you want to go the other way — hell, what's the use in arguing. I just go the way I want.

It took me a good half hour to make it back to the parish and another fifteen minutes before I pulled up in front of the St. Bernard Gun and Jewelry Shop. A guy with an orange crew-cut and an NRA tee-shirt told me I was a lucky guy. A week from now the Brady law goes into effect and I'd have to wait five days to get my gun.

Lucky for me, and unlucky for Coleman Hay, I walked out of the St. Bernard Gun and Jewelry Shop with a blue steel Smith & Wesson Model 15 Combat Masterpiece .38 caliber revolver. Snub-nosed with a two-inch barrel, I could carry it in my pocket. I bought a box of .38 'plus P' ammunition. I think the guy said 'plus P' meant plus power. Driving back into the city, I slipped six rounds into the cylinder. The checkered walnut stock felt so warm in my hand.

I caught the pain-in-the-ass St. Claude Avenue bridge, and was about to climb out of my car and put a couple slugs into the head of that goddamn bridge operator when a New Orleans police car pulled up behind me. So I just waited for twenty sweaty goddamn minutes for two ratty-looking tugs to chug through the locks from the river.

Closing my eyes, I could just see Coleman Hay's prissy face as I walk into his office and pull out the gun and point it between his beady eyes. His eyes grow wide. I squeeze the trigger until his head splits open like a melon. Then I put the gun down and wait for the cops and the media.

I could see the headlines — Playwright Slays Director of Downtown Arts Center. Beneath my picture would be the caption, "Yogi Bolds, whose plays were repeatedly rejected by the slain director, took out his revenge with a Smith & Wesson."

SURE, I'd spend some time in jail. I could use the time to write more plays, probably become the editor of that prison newspaper, the one touted on CNN. People won't forget my name. And one day I'll get out and Coleman Hay will still be dead.

A tap on the horn behind me brought me back to the bridge and the heat. I made sure I didn't break any traffic laws until after the cop car turned off on Desire Street. I made an illegal left turn at Franklin Avenue, just to piss off the other drivers, and took Chartres back to Piety Street.

I was in no special hurry. Coleman Hay never breezed into work until after "doing" lunch with an uptown snob or two. So I sat on my sofa, unloaded my Combat Masterpiece — God, what a great name for a gun — and dry-fired it. The slap of the hammer sounded nice and solid as it fell. I aimed it at the TV and it went click. I aimed it at the AC unit chugging in the window and it went click. I closed my eyes and aimed it between Coleman Hay's eyes and it went click.

Putting the Combat Masterpiece down, I went into my kitchen and pulled out the originals of my plays, all four of them, out of the refrigerator. Pulling them out of the extra-thick cardboard box, I laid them out on my bed so the cops would find them easily.

Then I went into my closet and pulled down the Xerox copies of my plays.

I found my phone book under the kitchen sink.

I found four unused envelopes, each big enough for a copy of each play, grabbed a red Bic pen and sat at my kitchen table. I addressed the envelopes to each of the three TV stations and one to *The Eagle* newspaper. Then I wrote four copies of the same note to put in each envelope. It said,

"Coleman Hay died because he was too stupid to stage these plays."

The kitchen clock read eleven o'clock.

I went back out to my sofa, sat down and closed my eyes and thought about my plays. Sweat rolled down my temples. I let it.

I pretended that I was being interviewed about killing Coleman Hay. That pretty blonde reporter from Channel 4 held a microphone in front of my face. So did that tall, skinny black guy from Channel 6 *and* that pretty black reporter from Channel 8, the one with the one long eye-brow across her forehead. I was handcuffed, but I could talk.

"Coleman Hay sent my first play back, saying he didn't find anything special in *The Huge, Sensitive German*. He actually said he didn't think a story about an ex-Nazi would capture an audience. Yeah? Well *Schindler's List* won the goddamn Academy Award.

"OK, so Schindler wasn't in the SS like my hero, but he was a party member. OK, so Schindler saved a lot of people. *My* hero ended up hating Hitler.

"Coleman Hay was even more brutal in rejecting my second play. He didn't even like the title, *Masticating Decatur Street*.

"What else could I name a story about a prostitute and a street cleaner?"

The pretty reporter with the long eye-brow would nod in agreement.

"He sent a form rejection slip when he rejected my third play, *Chartreuse Azaleas*. He didn't like the title either. *Steel Magnolias* — now that's a good title, but not *my* title.

"But the topper was my last play. He kept it six months before sending it back. How many times did I sit across the street from the Downtown Arts Center, on that broken concrete bench and dream about opening night?

"For the record, Coleman Hay rejected *Uptown Women in Beige con Mandingos,* a breakthrough play about race relations, for a piece of tripe called *Slimy Things Did Crawl With Legs Upon The Slimy Sea* written by a goddamn university professor. So what if it's a line from Coleridge, it's a dumb title."

My play clearly showed the guilt uptown white women feel toward black men because of slavery. The slimy play was *science-fiction.*

I looked at the clock. It was eleven-fifteen.

I got up and peeled off my shirt. I threw it against the wall and it stuck, it was so soaked. It slid down a moment later, leaving a wet mark on the wall and it occurred to me that I'll probably leave a red stain on Coleman Hay's pretty wallpaper.

I went in the bathroom and climbed out of my shorts and turned on the shower, then thought — what if the gun doesn't work? What if I pull it out, point it between those evil eyes, pull the trigger and it *doesn't* fire?

I hurried back into the front room, reloaded the Combat Masterpiece and brought it back to my bedroom. I grabbed my pillow, shoved it against the gun's muzzle and pointed the gun at my mattress. I squeezed the trigger until the gun fired. It was louder than I thought and kicked more than I thought.

My ears rang. The room smelled of burnt gunpowder and burned pillow. I put the gun on the bed next to my stories and took the pillow into the bathroom. I ran it under the faucet to put it out. It smoked pretty good.

Then I took my shower and put on a new Army-surplus green tee-shirt, brown jeans and my green and brown canvass authentic Vietnam jungle combat boots. The oil was back in my hair already, but I didn't give a damn.

I got six fresh cartridges and reloaded the Combat Masterpiece. I slipped it into the waistband of my jeans at the small of my back. Then I filled my pockets with the rest of the bullets and put on my favorite Khaki shirt to wear out over my tee-shirt to hide the gun. On my way out I grabbed my Cleveland Indians baseball cap and pulled it on my head.

I went the right way up Piety Street to Royal Street and took my time going through the Quarter, looking at the multi-colored buildings and the black balconies and the painted women and overweight men wearing the wrong colors. Finally leaving the Quarter, I drove through the central business district and into the warehouse district, thinking this city has too many goddamn districts.

At exactly one o'clock I parked my car next to a meter at the corner of Poeyfarre and Constance Street, climbed out and stretched. I reached around to adjust the gun in my waistband and it felt wet. I was soaked with sweat and nervous as hell, but I was happy.

I walked around to the side of the Downtown Arts Center and spotted Coleman Hay's white Mercedes parked in its reserved parking spot. I went back around to the front of the old red brick building and went in the front door. I took the elevator up to the reception area and breezed passed the receptionist who was too busy yakking on the phone to even look up.

Coleman Hay's pretty blonde private secretary pulled her

tight yellow skirt down, like she always does when I come in, crossed her legs and asked if I had an appointment.

"Not today," I said in a low, mousy voice. Looking down, all humble and all, I said, "I was hoping I could talk to Mr. Hay for a minute, if it's not too much to ask." Backing away from her desk, I pointed to one of the waiting chairs. "I'll just sit here, if you don't mind."

"Suit yourself," she said. "It's going to be a while. Mr. Coleman has a full slate."

"I'll wait."

She snapped her gum at me and went back to filing her nails. She never looked me in the eye, ever. She always wore tight skirts and always looked just past me when she had to talk to me.

I'd planned to just walk past her, right into Coleman's office, but just as I'd walked up to her desk I thought, "What if he's not in there? What if he's down the hall? What if he's in the men's room?"

I wiped the sweat from my face and sat as still as I could. I closed my eyes and thought about — *Uptown Women in Beige con Mandingos*. I could see Muffy Rosenberg-St. Cyr standing on the rear deck of her uptown home. Watching the tall, black gardener who is shirtless as he cuts her grass, her mouth trembles as she exclaims, "The guilt. The guilt. The guilt!"

Facing the gardener, Muffy unbuttons her blouse and pulls off her brassiere to expose her breasts to the gardener and says, "I can no longer live with the guilt in my breast. Look at me. Look, as I stand half-naked in front of your eyes. Cleanse the guilt from me!"

The gardener stands his ground proudly. Sweat covering

his massive brown chest, he looks at her heaving breasts with appreciation.

Now *that's* race relations

It's such a haunting scene, it made me tremble as I sat in the chair outside Coleman Hay's office.

The secretary got on the phone. Her head turned around to keep me from hearing she talked about someone being really depressed lately. I couldn't tell who it was, not that I gave a damn. The way she was turned, I could see the line of her body and it looked pretty good. Then I felt acid in my stomach, knowing Coleman Hay was probably nailing her.

I tried to keep calm, but my left arm started shaking and I couldn't keep my feet still. They kept wiggling. I knew she was going to turn around, see me all hyped-up and never let me in to see Coleman Hay. Only she kept talking on the phone, kept her back to me as the sweat poured down from my head. I licked it away from my lips and it tasted salty.

I closed my eyes again and waited.

I'VE BEEN WAITING HERE SO LONG I'm completely drenched, but she doesn't look at me, so she doesn't notice.

The clock over her head says it's now two o'clock.

She's reading a magazine now. *Cosmopolitan.* Someone comes in and she looks up.

It's another blonde woman in a big hurry. A fur piece around her shoulders, this one's taller and skinner and waves at the secretary as she rushes right into Coleman's office.

The secretary shrugs and snaps her gum again. I hate that.

I'm thinking, maybe I'll shoot her first when a man comes in, so quickly and quietly I don't see him until he's past me. He's big and wears a suit and looks a little like the guy who played Schindler in the movie.

The secretary says, "Excuse me."

The man yanks Coleman Hay's chrome-metal door open, slamming it against the wall on his way in.

The secretary rises, pushes her skirt down, snaps her gum and sits again.

I'm definitely shooting her on my way out, if she's stupid enough to still be here.

I hear loud voices coming from Coleman Hay's office. The secretary looks up and someone shouts, "No! No!". Then gun shots erupt in Coleman Hay's office, a bunch of shots. Eight I think, or nine.

The secretary jumps up. I stand and reach around for the Combat Masterpiece. The checkered grips are so wet, they're too slippery to hold. I wipe my hands on the chair just as the door crashes open again. The big guy moves through the doorway, a large automatic pistol in his right hand.

He takes two steps toward the secretary, stops, raises the gun to his temple and fires. He falls straight down and the secretary screams and runs out. I pull out the Combat Masterpiece and nearly drop it, it's so slippery. I hold it in a two-handed police stance, bend my knees and move past the body and through the doorway. I gotta make sure Coleman Hay's dead.

The blonde lies in front of the desk, her face a bloody pulp. Coleman Hay is in his high-back chair behind his enormous black lacquer desk. There are two holes in his forehead, a bloody mass gobbed along the back of his chair. It's hardcore, man.

He's dead I feel my heart stammering.

Then I hear voices outside.

I raise the Combat Masterpiece and aim it between Coleman Hay's eyes.

The voices are right outside now.

I have to move quickly to the door, and ease behind it as it opens. Two men rush in. I follow the swing of the door out, jump over the big guy's body and walk right out without so much as anyone even seeing me. I remember to uncock the Combat Masterpiece and slip it back under my shirt. There's a parking ticket on my windshield. I tear it up and toss it in the air.

I feel so good, I do a dance, a little jig next to my car. Then I see two police cars pull up and park haphazardly in front of the D.A.C., four officers rushing inside the building.

I'm no genius, but I'll bet Coleman was nailing the big guy's wife and got caught. Yep. That had to be it. I climb into my Datsun and pull away, resisting the urge to pump a few rounds into the police cars as I pass by. I catch a couple lights, still feeling pretty good, remembering the holes in Coleman Hay's head. I think, now the D.A.C. will get a new director and I'll finally see an opening night.

I weave through the streets, whistling. Then I get stuck in a traffic jam from hell on Decatur Street, so I turn up St. Louis, but it takes me nearly an hour to get to Rampart Street. I'm pissed again and hot as hell again and it occurs to me, what do I do now?

What if the next director doesn't see the light? What if he rejects my plays too? In my heart, I know he will. He'll be from uptown and drive a Mercedes and wear nice suits and hump blondes and only put on plays written by his friends.

What do I do? Go through all those rejections again, then kill him?

I think of the holes in Coleman Hay's head, but it doesn't give me the lift I'm looking for now.

I could . . . no . . . wow . . . I got it I look out of my car window up at the sky. I've been inspired — a heavenly inspiration. I pull against the curb and sit there a minute, my hands shaking. My plan can still work.

What the hell was I thinking? Coleman Hay was nobody. I'm gonna kill somebody *famous*.

ROBERT JESCHONEK

Robert Jeschonek continues his streak of being in every issue of this magazine.

The reason Robert has this streak is simply because his stories are often just perfect Pulphouse stories. Take this story, for example. Not a chance could I begin to describe it, and thus a perfect Pulphouse story.

Robert's stories have appeared in dozens of magazines and he has published dozens of novels as well. He has even worked for DC Comics and early in his career sold me a couple stories when I was editing for Star Trek at Pocket Books. He seems to be able to do it all. And to see all the amazing projects he has done, check out his website at https://www.robertjeschonek.com/

COCK-A-DOODLE-DIE

ROBERT JESCHONEK

S had Lum Lugo the meemee exterminator strutted across the paved lot, feeling the bright morning sun as it heated his feathers. He was glad to be alive, and he crowed about it again, though he'd already crowed at dawn as he did every day. Life, oh life was so *good*.

Then, suddenly, two meemees ran out of the brush in front of him, and he reared back, scrambling to aim his pistol at them.

The meemees were barely two feet tall, covered in fur (one black, one blond), and bipedal. It was the only thing they seemed to have in common with Shad's people, the Ch'Kaw-- getting around on two legs.

Otherwise, the meemees didn't measure up. The Ch'Kaw were ten feet tall, immeasurably smarter, covered with beautiful plumage, and the dominant species of planet Earth.

So why were the damned meemees so hard to *kill*?

They were fast on their feet, for one thing. Even as Shad

swung his pistol around, they scurried further away, heading for the back of The Coop restaurant. A few more steps, and the pistol would be useless; Shad couldn't open fire if there was a chance of hitting a worker inside the place.

So he took a chance and threw two shots at the fleeing meemees. Neither bullet hit its mark.

Then the meemees reached the restaurant and flung themselves into a tiny hole at the base of the wall. Shad had never noticed it before--but of course the damned meemees went straight for it.

Crowing with rage, Shad threw open the back door and charged into the building. From experience, he knew where the meemees would go, so he made a beeline for the kitchen.

Sure enough, they were up on a counter, heads submerged in a bowl of corn flour. As soon as he rushed in, they both looked up, furry faces dusted with pale yellow flour--then sprinted away, grabbing handfuls of corn biscuit crumbs from a tray en route.

"Vermin!" Shad didn't dare shoot up the kitchen, so he grabbed a metal skillet with one claw and heaved it at the meemees.

The creatures dove off the counter and landed on their feet on the blue-tiled floor. The skillet clanged off the counter and bounced down after them, but they were already racing away by then.

"I'll peck you to shreds!" howled Shad as he chased them. His razor-sharp beak could do some serious damage.

"*Mee mee mee mee mee!*" That was the sound the meemees made as they scrambled away from him and headed for the kitchen door. "*Mee mee mee mee mee!*" It was the cry that had given them their name once upon a time.

Shad knew they were heading for their bolt hole. He had to cut them off, or he might not get another chance at stopping their escape.

It was time for a bold move. Taking two big steps, he pushed off in a flying leap, aiming the claws of his feet at the fleeing pests. He might just take them both at once, if...

But no. The meemees darted through the kitchen doorway before he could nail them. Shad came down on his heels and slid, dropping hard on his ass.

A shock of pain jolted his spine, and he shrieked. As he slumped against the wall, he heard the meemees' hairy little feet pattering down the hall toward their escape hole.

And that made him shriek even louder.

———

"WHAT NEXT?" The white-feathered female was furious, clacking her beak against Shad's. "Are you going to *carry* the meemees in and *feed* them by *claw*?"

Shad shook his head with quick flicks, careful not to leave an opening for her sharp beak. Just because they were standing in the restaurant's dining room in view of several customers didn't mean she wouldn't jab his eye out. "Of course not, Lady Nixa."

"You might as well!" snapped Nixa. "You already *let* them come and go as they *please*!"

At her sharp, shrill tone, all the customers looked up at once, heads flicking and bobbing with interest. Then, they all returned to pecking away at the plates of fried worms and cornmeal biscuits on the tables in front of them.

"I can *do* the *job!*" Shad reared up with indignation, but he had to be careful. Lady Nixa owned the restaurant and was paying his fee--a fee he couldn't afford to lose.

"So you keep saying." Nixa lunged at him, then jerked away at the last second. The low red comb on top of her head quivered with rage. "But if I don't see results soon, you're *fired*, you washed-up loser."

"I'll *get* those meemees, don't you worry!" Shad crowed for emphasis.

"Big talk, cock," said Nixa. "Now walk the walk." She clucked with disgust. "If you can."

As SHAD CHECKED the cage traps in the parking lot, he got more and more angry. Not only had he not caught a single meemee, but every last bit of bait he'd planted had been spirited away.

The little bastards were tricky as hell and hard to kill. Not that Shad had gone after many of them before now. Actually, this was his first job as an exterminator, though he'd never tell Nixa that.

He'd thought it would be much easier. He'd only ever killed another Ch'Kaw before, in the cockfighting ring, and that hadn't been so hard...for a while, anyway.

But the meemees, it turned out, were much more of a challenge. He'd already been after them for three days, and the closest he'd come to contact was the chase he'd just had through the kitchen.

"Well, hello there." A strange voice interrupted his reverie. "Coming up empty, huh?"

Turning, Shad saw an elderly male limping toward him with a cane, bobbing his head. Immediately, Shad put down the latest trap and straightened. "What's it to you?"

"These traps won't work." The male swung his cane out and rapped it on the trap at Shad's feet. "Not for damned meemees. You're pecking at the wrong feed, friend."

"What do *you* suggest, Grampa?" Shad twitched his head, giving his comb and wattles a sarcastic shake.

"Name's Varn, not Grampa." Varn twitched his own head, but his shriveled comb and wattles didn't shake much. "And shame on you, if you think I'm dumb enough to tell you my meemee-killing tactics without a piece of the action."

Shad crowed with laughter and strutted away. "Get lost, old rooster." His high, purple tail feathers flickered as he walked. "You won't get any money out of me."

"Too bad." Varn made a rumbling noise deep in his throat--a Ch'Kaw sigh. "I was going to pay *you* to let me *help*."

Shad stopped strutting and whirled. "But you said you wanted a piece of the action."

"Exactly." Varn cluck-chuckled and flapped his arms. "The *action*, friend. The *killing*. I'm retired and *bored*."

Now Shad was interested. Keeping his head high, he scratched the pavement with his feet. "You say you have meemee-killing tactics?"

"*Scientifically developed* tactics." Varn chuckled again. "And cash money up front, friend." He reached between the dull gray feathers on his belly and drew out a clawful of glittering gold pellets.

Shad considered it for a moment, then shrugged. What did he have to lose? "Sure. Why not?"

Varn's feathers were thin, with the skin underneath showing through in patches, but he ruffled them excitedly anyway. "To murder most fowl!" And then he managed a hoarse crow that broke down into a ragged coughing jag.

"Voila!" Varn pulled an item out of a burlap sack--a tiny, rectangular object with curved corners, black all around. "The perfect bait!"

Shad flicked his head to the side and stared at the object with one eye. "What the hell is it?"

"An ancient artifact, dug up from deep underground." Varn turned the object around in his clawed hand, letting the sun glint off its smooth surface. "A remnant of a different age."

Dropping it in the bag, he headed across the parking lot toward the garbage pile in the far back corner.

Shad shook his head. "And it's supposed to be bait how?"

"The Ch'Kaw did not always rule the Earth," said Varn. "You know that, don't you?"

"I've heard theories."

"*More* than theories. *Facts.*" Varn shook his cane for emphasis. "This world was once dominated by a species calling itself 'Peeple.' How do we know this?" He held up the burlap sack. "*Evidence*, buried long, long ago."

When they got to the garbage pile, Shad spotted a swarm of bugs on some rotten cornbread and pecked them up. "If these Peeple were so dominant, what happened to them?"

"No one knows for sure." Varn pulled the black object from his sack and squatted down in front of the pile. "But the meemees look an awful lot like the Peeple did."

Shad stopped pecking at bugs. "The meemees?"

"Sure," said Varn. "Just much smaller, with bigger eyes. You've heard of evolution, haven't you? Creatures changing to adapt to their environment?"

"I guess so," said Shad.

Varn reached into his sack and fished around. "Some scientists think the Peeple changed over hundreds of thousands of years, becoming the meemees."

Shad let loose a sharp crow of laughter. "The same scientists who think the *Ch'Kaw* evolved from *birds?*"

"Don't laugh. There's plenty of evidence down there." Varn pointed his beak at the ground.

"Whatever." Shad shrugged. "It doesn't matter what came first, as long as we're the ones doing the killing."

"Indeed." Varn pulled a crescent-shaped metal object from the sack and put it down with a clank. "And this will do the job nicely, friend."

Shad recognized the object as a spring-loaded foot trap. He hadn't thought to bring one himself; he hadn't thought he'd need anything other than a couple of cage traps.

"Let's get this loaded." Varn opened the trap wide on the pavement and locked it by turning a key on its base. Gingerly, he lowered the black artifact inside, placing it on a pressure-sensitive metal plate. Then, he withdrew his claw and turned the key to unlock the trap. "Now, all we have to do is wait."

Shad frowned and twitched his head. "I don't understand how this bait will lure them in. What kind of artifact *is* it?"

Varn chuckled as he got to his feet. "If translations of the ancient texts are correct, Peeple called it a 'fone.' Some kind of communication device, apparently."

"They can use it to communicate?"

"Heavens no." Varn chuckled again. "It doesn't *work*. But they won't be able to keep their hands off it." He shrugged. "That's the theory, anyway."

"What if they don't *take* the bait?"

Varn shook his burlap sack, making the contents clank and jingle. "We've got lots more where *that* came from."

———————

BY THE TIME Varn had finished setting traps, the back parking lot was a kill zone for meemees. There were four traps around the trash pile, two up against the back wall of the restaurant, and six more ringing the edge of the lot.

To keep unwitting customers from getting hurt, Shad blocked off the back lot with yellow traffic cones. He also closed the area to all employees, though he knew he couldn't keep it that way for long.

Then, he and Varn pitched a black tent in the middle of the lot and waited inside, watching the traps through peepholes in the canvas.

"So," said Varn. "What made you want to get into the exterminator business?"

"Time for a career change, I guess." Shad squinted through one peephole, then moved on to the next. So far, he could see no action along the trap line.

"A change from what kind of career?" pressed Varn. "What did you do before this?"

Shad grunted. How many awful conversations had started with the same or similar words? He hated the thought of another--but lying his way out of it never seemed to be the answer. Sooner or later, the truth always caught up with him.

"A cockfighter," he said finally. "I was a cockfighter before this."

"Pro?" asked Varn.

"Yes," said Shad. "I was on the pro circuit."

"And your name is?"

"Shad Lum Lugo. But my pro name was Slaughterbeak."

"Slaughterbeak, huh?" Varn flashed him a look, then went back to staring out a peephole. "When was your last fight?"

"Six months ago," said Shad. "Against the Crimson Spurslasher."

"Sounds like quite an opponent," said Varn. "So why did you quit the fight game?"

Maybe now was the time for a lie or two. "I wanted to quit while I was still on top...and still in one piece." Shad didn't mention that he'd been forced out; why bring it up if the old rooster didn't know the story?

Luckily, Varn didn't seem to pick up on the fib. "Sounds like a smart move, friend. You saved your own skin and cleared the way for new talent in the bargain, didn't you?"

Shad moved to another peephole. "You read my mind, Varn."

Varn started to say something, then stopped and leaned closer to his own peephole. "Here we go now. Vermin on the march, Slaughterbeak."

Shad darted over to a peephole on the same side of the tent as Varn's. Sure enough, three meemees had scampered out of the brush and were approaching the traps by the garbage pile.

"Watch this." Varn chuckled. "Little buggers won't be able to resist the bait we put out."

At first, it looked like he'd be right. The meemees--a black-furred male, a blonde female, and a red-furred male child--went straight to the trap with the fone and circled it several times.

But they didn't take the bait. Instead, they moved on to the next trap.

"Don't worry," said Varn. "They're as good as dead."

The next trap was baited with a stack of what Varn had called "credicards"--thin pieces of plastic that had once been used for financial transactions. That was the theory, anyway.

The meemees crept around the spring-loaded trap, eyes fixed on the stack of cards. They sniffed at them, taking the scent from beyond the trap's reach. They gestured and babbled to each other...but they never made a move to enter the trap. And then they moved on.

Varn clucked angrily. "Come on, come on." He ruffled his sparse gray feathers and rapped the pavement with his cane. "I *know* they can't pass up the *next* bait."

The third trap held a gleaming bar of solid gold. As with the first two traps, the meemees circled around it, staring and sniffing--and then they stopped. The adults stood straight, cupped their furry hands around their mouths, and cried out.

"*Mee mee mee mee!*" Small as they were, their voices carried well across the parking lot and beyond. "*Mee mee mee mee mee!*"

"What are they doing?" said Shad.

Just as the words left his mouth, a horde of meemees poured out of the jungle and swarmed the parking lot. There were dozens of them, and they weren't empty-handed.

Every last meemee of every age, size, and fur color was carrying a rock or a stick.

Shad sucked in his breath. Were the rocks and sticks meant to be used as tools or weapons?

The answer was "tools." As the meemees charged out of the jungle brush, they used the rocks and sticks to trigger the traps. When the traps sprung, the bait was ejected, clattering to the pavement.

Instantly, the meemees scooped up the bait and dashed away on their tiny, furry feet. They scattered in all directions, carrying off fones and credicards, gold bars and carkees and wristclocks. As they ran, the air was filled with their high-pitched cries. "*Mee mee mee mee mee mee mee!*"

Shad hissed a curse and bolted out of the tent. He grabbed the pistol from the holster at his waist and waved it around, trying to pick a target...but it wasn't easy. He'd never seen so many meemees in one place before, and they were all moving fast. Carefully drawing a bead on one was out of the question. Better to shoot randomly into the herd; he was bound to hit something that way.

But just as he had that thought, something locked up inside him. Instead of pouring bullets into warm meemee bodies, he froze as the creatures scampered away from him.

"What the hell?" Just then, Varn lurched out of the tent. "Shoot! They're getting away!"

Shad thought fast. "Not yet! This is our chance!"

"Chance for what, you chickenshit?"

"To follow them," said Shad. "To find their nest. Then we can stop them once and for all."

"Not a bad idea." Varn bobbed his head and managed a

hoarse crow. "Let's turn their home sweet home into the world's biggest meemee burial ground."

SHAD AND VARN left the restaurant behind and followed the meemees into the jungle. Shad stayed out ahead--he had to, to keep the meemees in sight--but he tried not to lose the slower-moving old-timer in the process.

The mid-day heat was high, the humidity thick as soup all around, but Shad didn't mind. He lived for warmth and sunlight; he'd always been a hot-blooded type...and not just when it came to climate. He loved the heat that came with action and excitement, too, the way it got his blood pumping harder and made him feel truly alive. It was what he'd loved most about his cockfighting days, even after he'd lost his edge.

Not that he'd see much action if the meemees got away...which they might. Hanging back because of Varn, Shad could just make out the tops of some of the creatures' furry heads in the distant brush. If the meemees managed to get much further away, he would lose them altogether.

Though, truth be told, he wasn't confident of succeeding in his mission even if he did catch up to them. Fear coiled in the back of his mind like a snake...fear that he'd blow this hunt the same way he'd blown his cockfighting career.

And for the same reason, too.

"Hold up!" Varn's voice rang out from far behind--much farther behind than Shad would have expected. "Slow down a little!"

It was the exact opposite of what Shad wanted to do, but

losing the old rooster might not help his cause. Grudgingly, he stopped and waited, watching the far-off heads of the meemees get even farther off.

"Thanks." Varn was out of breath as he hobbled up through the brush. "I guess...I can't run...through the jungle...like I used to."

"No problem." Shad kept watching the meemees, who were almost out of sight. "But we've got to keep moving."

Varn nodded and sighed. "I will, I will."

"We're losing them!" Shad couldn't see the meemees anymore, just the brush rustling in their wake.

"So follow...their tracks." Varn poked Shad's side with his cane to get his attention, then jabbed the cane at the ground.

Sure enough, the jungle mud was full of tiny footprints. Shad recognized them instantly as meemee tracks: each had five toes joined to an oblong foot, concave on the inside, deeper at the ball and heel.

"See?" Varn cluck-chuckled. "As long as we still have daylight, we can follow the trail."

"Good." Shad nodded with quick flicks of his head. "But let's keep up the best we can anyway. These things can be damned tricky."

"Their ancestors ruled the world for thousands of years," said Varn. "I guess some of that had to stay with them."

TIME PASSED, and Shad and Varn kept moving. There was always plenty of fresh trail to follow--tiny prints and occasional droppings in the mud. Once in a while, Shad even glimpsed rippling brush or a furry scalp in the distance. Sometimes, he heard faint "*mee mee mee*" cries piping through the jungle greenery.

But he didn't let it make him hurry. He maintained a slow and steady pace, which Varn seemed to appreciate.

Instead of gasping for breath, the old-timer was able to carry on a conversation as he hiked...though Shad only half listened to what he was saying.

"It's funny what evolution can do." Varn said it as Shad helped him across a stream. "The rulers of the world, the Peeple, become the humble little meemees, scavenging to survive and running for their lives."

"If you say so." Shad tested a rock in the middle of the stream, decided it was steady, and put his full weight on it. Then, he pulled Varn after him and stepped from the rock to the bank.

"The Peeple had a theory, too, you know," said Varn. "They believed that millions of years before Peeple came along, the world was ruled by giant beasts called 'dinosaurs.' What do you suppose became of them?"

Shad was more interested in pulling Varn to the bank and picking up the meemees' trail, which he was having trouble finding. "Killed off by the Peeple?"

"Not at all, friend. The Peeple believed that the dinosaurs *evolved*. Over millions and millions of years, they shrank and became *birds*. But here's the most interesting part."

"I'm listening," said Shad as he walked along the bank with his head bobbing low, looking for tracks in the mud.

"According to *modern* scientists, certain birds evolved into *us*." Varn sounded excited. "Birds, descended from the dinosaur rulers of the world, again became the rulers of the world as the *Ch'Kaw*. And the Peeple shrank and became the tiny, pesky meemees. What goes around, comes around, eh?"

"Ah-ha!" Shad let out a crow of victory. The meemees must have waded downstream a few yards before leaving the water...but he'd found their fresh tracks anyway, stamped in the muddy bank and trailing off into the brush.

"Kind of makes you wonder what's next," said Varn, lingering along the stream for a moment before realizing he was alone and hobbling off to catch up with Shad.

A LITTLE FURTHER ALONG, the meemee tracks led Shad to a clearing, about twenty yards across. He paused at the edge of it, looking around at the mat of flattened grass spanning the open space.

Suddenly, he heard familiar, high-pitched cries piping up. "*Mee mee mee mee mee!*" Six meemees leaped out from behind bushes and tree trunks on the opposite side, waving fones and credicards and carkees.

"Damned things." Glancing over his shoulder, he saw Varn draw up behind him. "I'll be right back."

Varn bobbed his head, looking confused. "But I..."

Shad didn't wait for him to finish his sentence. Grabbing his pistol from the holster, he charged into the clearing, eyes fixed on the screeching meemees.

Adrenaline burned through his arteries, and his heart hammered as he ran. The meemees hopped up and down and waved their toys, egging him on with their screeches. Clearly, they wanted him to keep charging straight for them.

But why? Why the hell would they want that?

Suddenly suspicious, Shad slowed near the middle of the clearing...and the ground gave way under his right foot. He stopped just in time, stumbling back as the mat of flattened grass dropped away in front of him, revealing a gaping pit.

Crowing with alarm, he staggered back. One step further forward, and he would've plunged right into the hole.

"*Mee mee mee mee mee!*" On the far side of the clearing, the meemees were jumping around like maniacs. Their screeches were shrill with rage; they hurled their toys at Shad and hurled globs of feces to go with them.

Steadying himself, Shad swung up the pistol and pointed it in the meemees' direction. When one of their fones bounced off his chest, he cocked the gun and got ready to fire.

One of the meemees, a silver-haired male, was in Shad's sights. All he had to do was pull the trigger.

Which he did...but only after swinging the pistol to point straight up in the air, leaving the meemees unharmed.

Angry screeches changing to frightened ones, the meemees bolted off into the dense brush. They were gone in a flurry of foliage, leaving Shad standing alone in the clearing.

"What the hell?" Easing up to the edge of the pit, he saw it was at least twelve feet to the bottom--deep enough to contain him. "They tried to *trap* me?"

Varn limped up beside him. "Sure looks that way, friend."

"But meemees don't *do* that," said Shad. "They don't *do* that to Ch'Kaw."

"They do now."

Shad gaped at the fluttering brush in the distance. "But they're not that *smart*, are they?"

"Like I told you." Varn patted his shoulder. "Used to rule the *planet*, friend."

AFTER THE INCIDENT in the clearing, Shad and Varn continued onward, following the meemees' tracks.

Shad moved more cautiously now, worried that the meemees might try something else. It didn't seem likely, but their first attempt at trapping him hadn't seemed likely, either.

One question stuck in his mind: If the meemees were smart enough to dig a hole, cover it over, and lure him into it, what else might they be capable of?

At least he wasn't tracking them alone--though Varn seemed more concerned about Shad than he was about the meemees.

"Why carry that gun?" asked Varn as they worked their way up a hill. "You haven't used it much, have you?"

Shad jerked his head around, comb and wattles quivering, and glared at him. "I've used it *plenty*."

"You're good at waving it around, all right." Varn grunted as he pushed off with his cane, taking another step up the hillside. "Good at shooting it straight up in the air, too. But I have yet to see you nail a meemee with that sidearm of yours."

"Haven't seen *you* get one, either," snarled Shad. "What happened to those scientifically-developed tactics you were running your mouth about?"

Varn ignored the remark. "What's your malfunction, friend? Are you gun-shy in general, or just when it comes to shooting meemees?"

Shad whirled and lunged, ending up beak-to-beak with Varn--but the old-timer didn't back down. He just kept looking at Shad expectantly.

For a moment, Shad was seized by the urge to attack, to give Varn an old-fashioned peck-down straight out of the cockfighting ring. But then he remembered how he'd changed since his days in the fight game; a single flash of anger couldn't undo all that.

Which was kind of the old-timer's point. Shad wasn't the same rooster he'd once been.

As the anger drained out of him, Shad bobbed his head and backed away. "One of the reasons I'm doing this," he said, "is to fire up my killer instinct again."

"So *that's* why you left cockfighting." Varn nodded. "You lost your *bloodlust*."

"It's still there." Shad glared at him with one baleful brown eye. "It just needs a jump-start."

"But the meemees aren't doing it for you, are they?" Varn twitched his head from side to side. "Why is that?"

Shad's impulse was to deny there was any problem at all...but he fell silent instead.

"They're filthy, disease-ridden pests," said Varn. "Why hold back from blowing them away whenever possible?"

Shad opened his beak to speak...but before he could say anything, he was distracted by a familiar cry in the distance.

"*Mee mee mee mee mee mee mee!*"

The sound was coming from up the hill. Looking toward it, Shad saw twelve meemees on the crest of the hill, silhouetted against the deep blue afternoon sky.

Feeling compelled to prove himself, Shad let out a wild crow and charged toward the row of meemees. He heard Varn shouting something behind him, but he couldn't make it out and didn't care. It was time to blow through the barriers holding him back; it was time to kill some damned meemees.

As he ran closer, the meemees grew more agitated. They threw fones and gold bars and artifacts he didn't recognize, pitching them in his direction with frenzied shrieks.

Shad just kept charging. He drew his pistol and cocked the hammer, determined to plug all twelve meemees if he could.

Then, he felt something snap against his ankle--something like a stiff vine...or a wire. Stopping in his tracks, he spotted a sudden blur of movement from the corner of his eye and looked left. That was when he saw a huge object hurtling toward him, coming in fast.

Instinctively, he threw himself down. He hit the ground

just in time as the flying object swooped over him, so close it buzzed off a few feathers, and kept going.

Looking up in its wake, Shad saw what it was: a log, suspended in some kind of harness, swinging between the trees. If it had hit him, he had no doubt it would have killed him.

He must have triggered it when he stepped through the wire. It could not have been a coincidence that the meemees had been egging him on in that direction.

They had set a second trap. And this time, they had come even closer to killing him.

SHAD AND VARN CONTINUED ONWARD, following the trail more cautiously than ever. As they forged ahead, the sun moved lower in the sky, shifting the day ever closer to evening.

"We're running out of daylight," said Shad as he ducked under low-hanging vines in an especially dense patch of jungle. "Maybe we ought to turn around."

Varn shot off a little crow of contempt. "Typical. This is just like your last match against the Crimson Spurslasher back in '27."

Shad's head pivoted to fix the old-timer in a stunned glare. "I thought you didn't know who I was before today! I thought you hadn't followed my career!"

"I never said that." Varn shrugged. "Who *hasn't* heard the story of *Slaughterbeak*? You were one of the all-time *greats* until you started *choking* and got put out to *pasture*."

Shad felt betrayed. The old-timer didn't sound much like a

friend anymore. "Shut your beak. You don't know anything about that world." Turning to face forward, he resumed pushing through the vines and brush.

Varn laughed. "I know more than you think!"

Shad's blood was boiling as he thrashed his way through a tangle of leafy vines. When he'd cleared them, he found himself gazing at a strange sight.

Some kind of structure lay before him, a waist-high white altar rising from the jungle floor. It looked as if it were built from thousands of white pieces--some curved, some jagged, some knobby, some flat. The closer he looked, the more clearly it came into focus, and he realized what exactly the pieces were.

Bones. They were bones.

Shad twitched and shuddered. "Time to turn around."

But when he took a step back, he bumped into Varn. "That would be rude, friend." Varn cluck-chuckled and nudged Shad forward with the tip of his cane. "They've been expecting us."

Just then, Shad heard rustling sounds from the brush. A familiar call, faint at first, drifted up all around him.

"*Mee mee mee mee mee mee mee.*"

"Expecting us?" Shad's voice had a nervous hitch to it. "What makes you think that?"

Varn leaned up close to Shad and whispered in his ear. "Because I told them we were coming. I told them I was going to introduce them to my son's very special friend who was dying to meet them."

Shad swallowed hard. Reaching down, he slid his pistol from its holster. "Who's your son?"

Varn leaned even closer and hissed his next words. "The

Crimson Spurslasher. Remember him?" He gave Shad a sharp peck on the back of the head. "You know what happens when you refuse to administer the kill shot to an opponent in the ring, don't you? The way you refused to kill the Crimson Spurslasher in the last bout of your career?"

Shad tightened his grip on the pistol in his left claw. "Disgrace."

"For starters," said Varn. "The loser left alive is seen as a failure and coward who ought to be dead. No one will fight him, because the only thing more disgraceful than being spared in the ring would be *losing* to someone who's been spared."

As Varn continued his story, the meemees' voices grew louder. Shad felt as if a huge door was closing behind him, and he didn't have long before it slammed shut for good.

"The disgraced fighter loses everything," said Varn. "He becomes a *laughingstock* and a *pariah*. More often than not, he is driven to take his own *life*...as indeed the Crimson Spurslasher did. And even then, his *family* knows no *peace*. All because of one act of *cowardice* by a gutless *cock* like *you*." Lunging forward, he pecked at the back of Shad's head with angry force.

Crowing with rage, Shad leaped away from him. The move took him close enough to the altar that he could make out what kind of bones had gone into its construction.

Ch'Kaw bones. Every bone he could see had come straight out of a dead Ch'Kaw.

Suddenly, the calls of the meemees got louder than ever. So did the rustling of the brush. All at once, the jungle parted, and hundreds of meemees poured forth.

This time, they weren't carrying fones, credicards, carkees, and the like. Some had rocks, and others had sharp sticks. As they closed in around Shad, he could see other objects scattered throughout the crowd--knives of all sizes clutched in tiny, furry hands, looking much too big for the little creatures who carried them.

Shad turned in a circle, scanning the crowd for a thin spot where he might break through. From what he could see, there was no such spot; if anything, the crowd kept expanding on all sides as more meemees ran in from the jungle.

"Here's where my scientifically-developed tactics come in," said Varn. "I haven't learned how to *kill* the meemees, but to *communicate* with them. And guess what?" He crowed with delight. "We found *common ground*."

Shad raised the pistol and pointed it at the crowd. Just then, the meemees started pelting him with a flurry of rocks.

"We both hate *chickens*!" said Varn, and then he roared with clucking laughter.

The flurry of rocks became a torrent, bombarding Shad from all sides. Sharp sticks hurtled among the rocks, piercing his skin like tiny spears.

Shad's clawed finger remained curled around the trigger of his pistol. He meant to fire, knowing full well it might be his best chance at survival...yet he still hesitated.

"Stop it!" He released a furious crow, the kind that had once terrified opponents in the ring--but the meemees kept attacking. "Get away from me!"

A big rock hit him on the back of the head, stunning him on impact. He wobbled, waving the gun one way and then the other, but his vision clouded, and he couldn't pick a target.

Then, a moment of clarity washed over him. He steadied, and his vision cleared. A black-furred meemee came into focus, gazing up at him with big, dark eyes.

Shad intended to kill it. Clenching his beak in concentration, he fixed the meemee in his gunsight. He steeled himself to murder that creature, hoping that one death might be enough to give the other meemees pause.

But at the last instant, he swung the gun up and fired at the treetops instead.

Why? That was what he thought as the crowd rushed in and brought him down with rocks and sticks and tiny, furry hands. *Why can't I bring myself to kill them?*

Shad swatted and struggled, but the meemees overwhelmed him. They bashed and stabbed him with their weapons and pinned him to the muddy ground.

Then, the meemees with knives leaped into the heart of the fray. Shad thrashed when he felt their cold blades slice into his throat, but he couldn't dislodge them. They just kept cutting and hacking, and he screamed the whole time.

Until they severed his windpipe, that is.

When they broke through his spine and lifted his head away from his body, Shad had the strangest sense of freedom. Ch'Kaw couldn't fly, but he felt at first as if indeed he were taking flight.

The meemees carried him up onto the altar. Peering over the edge, he could see his headless body on the ground--and then it broke free of the meemees pinning it down. Jumping up, the body raced in circles around the altar, knocking meemees out of the way of its headless, mindless charge.

But eventually, the meemees brought it back down. They

flung it on its back on the bone altar and pinned it there with the force of numbers.

Next, the meemees with the knives climbed up onto its chest and started cutting. They opened up the sternum and hacked out the V-shaped bone from the middle of the rib cage.

Then, as the mob chanted in unison...

"*Mee mee mee mee mee mee mee!*"

...two meemee males, both red-furred, took hold of the bone, one gripping each slender stem...

"*Mee mee mee mee mee mee mee!*"

...and they snapped it, breaking it into two uneven pieces...

"*Mee mee mee mee mee mee mee!*"

...and the one with the longer piece cheered, waving his piece of the bone in the air for all to see.

And that was when Shad faded, sliding away from the jungle and into somewhere else...taking only one thought with him on the journey. A question.

"*Why can't I bring myself to kill them?*"

"TELL me a story about the meemees, Mommy."

When Shad opened his eyes again, he was six weeks old--a tiny peep covered in yellow fuzz, hunkered down in the straw of his family's coop.

"If you insist." His mother sat in front of him, squatting on a clutch of eggs that had yet to hatch. Her pale feathers glowed in the bright moonlight streaming through the windows. "This one is called 'The Meemees and the Brave Little Peep.'"

Shad bounced in the straw and chirped with delight. His mother told him meemee stories every night; he could listen to them forever...or at least until he drifted off to sleep.

Shad's mother cleared her throat. "Once upon a time, there was a little peep who was afraid of the dark." She didn't need to read from a book; she knew all the stories by heart. "When clouds hid the moon, turning his room from bright to dark, he became very scared."

"What was the little peep's name?" asked Shad. "Was it the same as mine?"

"Yes, it was," said Mommy. "And little Shad shivered in the straw, unable to fall asleep. What if it was never light again?"

Shad listened with eyes wide and tiny heart racing. He knew exactly how the Shad in the story felt.

"Then, one night, three visitors flew in through the window." Mommy bobbed her head happily. "They were magical creatures, not much bigger than Shad was. Each had two arms, two legs, and two graceful gossamer wings like the wings of a butterfly. One was covered in red fur, one was covered in blond fur, and the other had jet black fur from head to toe."

"*Meemees!*" Shad let loose a high-pitched, chirping crow of excitement.

Mommy cocked her head to one side. "Very *special* meemees. *Meemee fairies.* The kind that flutter in through the window when little peeps are afraid of the dark. The kind that *light up* from inside with a soft, blue glow that comes straight from the love in their hearts."

"They *glow*?" said Shad.

"And the light from their hearts helps little peeps not be afraid of the dark anymore." Mommy let out a string of soft, loving clucks. "That's exactly what they did for little Shad that night. They flew around and played with him for hours, laughing and glowing in the darkness that wasn't so dark anymore."

"Then what happened?" said Shad.

LONG AFTER MOMMY had fallen asleep, Shad thought about the story she'd told him. It was his new favorite; he couldn't get it out of his head.

Eventually, he began to drift off. As he floated in the twilight gulf between consciousness and sleep, dreams mixed with reality in his young mind.

That was when he saw them, just as his mother had described. Three meemees fluttered in on gossamer wings, each one glowing with magic.

He giggled as they circled around him. They waved and beamed down at him with loving smiles, radiating warmth. They told him, without saying a word, that he had nothing to fear.

They played and frolicked there for hours, or what seemed like hours to a half-dreaming peep. They swooped low and tickled his belly, making him wriggle and twitter. They lifted him up in the air and danced with him, swinging him around with the greatest of ease.

Shad crowed and laughed until it hurt. Somehow, all the commotion never woke his mother on her clutch of eggs.

Then, the meemees joined hands around him in midair. He stayed aloft by flapping his fuzzy arms, hovering high above the straw in one glittering moonbeam.

At the end of Mommy's story, little Shad had become an honorary meemee. The same thing happened again, to the little Shad who'd listened to the story.

Glowing more brightly than ever, the meemees turned in a slow circle around Shad. Without saying a word, they swore him in as an honorary member of their order for life.

When they were done, Shad glowed as brightly as the meemees. From that moment on, some part of him would always be a part of them. Even if he forgot in the crush of a lifetime, in the blood and pain and strife of days heaped upon each other like logs on a bonfire, that night would leave its mark.

And one day, the story and dream might come back to him in full, swiveling out of the darkness like glowing winged meemees racing toward the moon in the last precious moments before the horizon swallows it up.

BRIAN THOMAS WOODS

Brian Thomas Woods is the second writer who has a first story in this issue.

As with K.A Wiggins, this story came through the stories sent by backers from the Pulphouse Fiction Magazine subscription drive. I started reading it and was instantly hooked in by the details and the incredible character voice.

And the story fits Pulphouse. So welcome, Brian.

MILK RUN

BRIAN THOMAS WOODS

The old Ford's yellow headlamps lit the road like a miserly torch bearer. Phil could hardly make out the twist and turns of the undulating asphalt. Tall pines lined either side of the two-lane road, looming above him, their needled peaks reaching up into the moonless night sky.

A Stompin' Tom song leaked out of the AM radio, Kawartha Lakes 1010, and the heater spued lukewarm air that smelled of burnt hair. Tom was singing about Margo and her cargo and her man Reggie having the rig. A true Canadian trucking classic if ever there was one.

Phil chewed on a piece of salty beef jerky, cranked up the heater and the burnt hair smell intensified. Nothing was a better barometer of an impending Ontario winter like that particular heater smell.

He glanced over to the passenger seat, took in the bags of milk he'd just purchased from McGovern's, the all-night

General Store, and sighed. There was some universal law that children must finish all the milk in the house and never mention it to anyone.

There was a second law that stated, wives must send their husbands out on milk runs no matter what time the lack of milk is discovered. So here he was, 3:00 am in the morning, driving down a deserted pitch-black road.

Living the dream.

He'd told his wife that the kids could do without milk in the morning.

"They need it for their cereal. We can't send them off to school on empty stomachs, can we?" Then she gave him that look.

He wasn't sure why they couldn't just eat toast and some fruit, but his wife wasn't having any of it and as usual she got her way.

One the plus side, it was a nice night for a drive on quiet roads. Just Phil and Stompin' Tom, two men singing about the hardships of life on the road carrying cargo for their ladies.

Phil cranked the Ford's heater up a little higher, blew into his hands to warm them up, the steering wheel was sending a chill directly into his bones and laughed when a gentle snow began to fall, as if summoned by his need for more heat.

The snow caught the light of the headlamps and made the big open road feel narrow and claustrophobic. It was like driving into a swirling vortex, a wormhole to travel unbelievable distances in a matter of minutes. And for a few minutes he imagined himself a traveler in space, the smell of burned hair the scent of an undiscovered planet's atmosphere. He imagined himself a brave explorer, visiting galaxy after galaxy and having adventure after adventure.

And when a deer jumped out in front of his car, stopped, and stared into his headlights, he snapped out his reverie and swerved the truck first to the left, just clipping the deer's chest, and then over corrected, steered all the way over to the right side of the road his tires sliding along the gravel edge before the truck came to a full stop.

His heart was beating like a war drum, his fingers had welded themselves to the steering wheel. He remembered to breathe, and then his body took back control and he was breathing too much, like a cat about to bring up a fur ball. He managed to loosen his grip on the steering wheel, his fingers peeled away like they had been glued there and shifted the truck into park.

The only coherent thought he could make was, 'Holy Shit, holy Shit!'

After what felt like an eternity he opened the door, stepped out of the truck, and looked back the way he had come. He could see serpentine black marks where he had swerved and braked at the same time. His eyes followed the lines back until he found the deer. It hadn't bothered to move.

It stood still. Staring at him. Like it had questions.

But the first ever human-deer dialogue was not to be. A noise came from the trees, Phil looked over the roof of his truck towards the area he thought the sound had originated from. He looked back to the deer, saw it bolt in the opposite direction and disappear back into the woods.

There it was again. He looked back across to where the sounds emanated. It was getting louder. More distinct. Like hundreds of twigs being snapped all at the same time. It was the oddest sound he had ever heard.

A bird flew out of the trees, wings flapping a hundred miles a minute, flew over his head and across the road. It sounded like a grouse. Then a murder of crows broke out of the trees a few hundred yards further down. They were unusually silent.

Phil stood with his mouth hanging open, snowflakes landing on his tongue. His mouth shut with a snap when a black bear emerged from the underbrush passing right in front of his truck. The bear made eye contact with him, let out a sound that Phil interpreted as robust displeasure, but otherwise paid Phil no heed, and continued into the brush across the road.

This was followed by a zookeeper's nightmare; all the animals had escaped and were attacking the city. Phil saw moose, elk, badgers, weasels, squirrels, and all manner of bird. He wouldn't have been surprised to see fish jumping across the road.

The noise of all these creatures became deafening. And yet not one of them took any interest in Phil.

His first thought was of forest fire. He sniffed the air for signs of smoke, but there wasn't any. His second thought jumped all the way to Sasquatch. It wasn't that he believed in them so much as that he didn't not believe in them.

And then it was quiet. Just like that he was alone in the chilly silence. It definitely felt a lot colder now. Phil walked around to the front of his truck to examine the bumper. He was worried the deer had damaged the bumper. It was getting harder to find replacement parts for the old truck and he loved the old girl. He'd inherited it from his father who had inherited it from his father.

The bumper and grill looked damage free. A tiny tuft of deer fir had been caught in the grill and a little smear of blood had been left behind, but that was the extent of the damage. He pulled the tuft off and walked over to the side of the road to throw it away.

As soon as he let it go a spotlight lit him up like an escaped convict. All he needed was some rookie deputy looking to bust him on littering charges. But there was no police car. The light came from above. He tried to look up at it, but it was so intense that it hurt the back of his eyes. He heard a faint humming noise. A low frequency hum like those old school fluorescent bulbs. He held his hand up to shade his eyes, the light pulsed brighter, and he yelled out in pain. The truck shut off and the headlights died.

The light was extinguished, the truck lights came back on, and Phil was surprised to find that he had dropped to his knees. The light and pain had lasted just a second, but his head hurt now. He felt like he was having a migraine attack. The snow melted and seeped into his pants, the damp chill ran rampant up and down his spine.

He remembered the deer, swerving to avoid it and wondered if he had imagined everything after that. Had he been in an accident and maybe hit his head? He wasn't sure. Everything was a little fuzzy and his head sure felt like it was going to split apart. He climbed back into the cab and closed the door. He just needed to sit for a moment and collect himself.

He started the truck, hungry for the heater's warmth. The smell of burning hair brought him back to the present. He adjusted the rearview mirror, then the side mirror. The seat felt too close to the steering wheel, so he adjusted the bench back a click. He took a deep breath and drove home at a pace that would have had senior drivers honking at him. Better safe than sorry.

———

BACK AT HOME, Phil put the milk in the fridge, popped a couple of extra strength pain killers and slipped into bed, doing his best not to disturb his wife. He was exhausted and fell into a deep slumber almost instantly.

He awoke to an empty bed. He rubbed his eyes and made the blurry time to be nine-ten AM. He'd slept in, his wife and kids were already at school and work. He felt robbed. The day had started without him, and he had not been able to tell the tale of his story to Marsha.

His head was still banging. So, he sent an email calling in

sick. He could use a day of rest, but soon found himself restless. He got out of bed and threw on a zippered hoodie and track pants. The hoodie felt a bit snug so decided a healthy breakfast was in order. At this age weight can sneak up on you. He'd eat healthily for the rest of the week and see if he could drop a few pounds. At least that was the idea. In practice he made himself a pot of coffee, with milk, because he earned that milk, a stack of pancakes drenched in syrup, two eggs, half a package of bacon and toast slathered in butter.

He was ravenous, so much so that the plates seemed too small, and the knife and fork felt like children's cutlery. He demolished his breakfast in short order and then went back to bed to watch daytime television.

On the way back to the bedroom he hit his head on the top of the doorframe. The headache transformed into a replica of the worst hangover he'd ever had and then it dawned on him. He'd hit the top of the door frame.... With his head!

Ducking low, Phil made his way into the bedroom and looked at himself in his wife's full-length mirror. He looked unbelievingly at his reflection. His five-nine frame was now easily six foot-seven. His hands were bigger, his fingers longer. He pulled his PJ's open and looked down below. Impressive. And weird. Not his thingy, well not just his thingy. He was just bigger all over.

None of this made any sense. Phil judged himself to have hit his head harder last night than he remembered. It was the only thing that really made any sense. He went back to bed and dreamt of Sasquatch chasing animals through the woodlands.

He woke up around two o'clock in the afternoon. He was ravenous again. He grabbed his runners and found he couldn't quite get his feet into them. He exchanged them for a pair of slip on flipflops and ducked his way through doors until he made it to his truck. The old girls' springs groaned as he dropped himself into the driver's seat. The need for food was all encompassing. Phil made tracks in the gravel driveway as he gunned the engine and sped out onto the tarmac road.

The closest place to get food was Churley's Chicken and Burgers. A Fifties diner style restaurant that once delivered your food to your car via roller-skated waitresses, but now had a convenient drive-thru option for modern eaters. He ordered enough food to feed his family twice over, paid and pulled the truck into one of the less conspicuous parking spaces along the back of the building. He ate everything. The thought made him sick and satisfied at the same time. He smelled of grease, chicken, and regret.

The meal, having satisfied his hunger pains, did what that kind of meal often did next, it put him to sleep.

———————

PHIL WOKE IN THE DARK. An advertisement for the local AA meeting had been stuck under his windshield wiper blade so he would see it upon waking. His body felt stiff. His muscles ached from sleeping in an awkward position. He realized his head touched the roof and was bent sideways while his knees were pinned under the steering wheel, he couldn't move his feet.

At first panic set in. Phil wondered again if he had been in some kind of car accident. But the surroundings were all wrong. He was still at Churleys. Empty wrappers and cups littered the passenger side bench. With some difficulty he maneuvered his left hand along the door panel until he found the handle. When he pulled it, the door sprang open, and his upper half fell out of the cab. His feet were stuck amongst the gas pedal and the brake. He kicked and wiggled his feet until they came free. He stood gingerly and leaned an elbow against the roof of his truck. It took him a moment to realize that should not be physically possible. The roof of the truck should be about at the height of his head. Here he was leaning on it with his elbow.

He'd grown again.

The first time was after the thing in the sky. The second was after he'd had breakfast and now this third after he'd gorged on fried chicken.

Eat, Sleep, Grow.

He looked over to the diner and saw all the patrons staring at him through the window. They looked like they were scared. Twenty or thirty cellphones were aimed at him like pistols. Each one taking a shot.

A serpentine line of silent police cars wound their way into the parking lot circling his truck. Flashing Red and blue lights turned the place into a disco. Phil looked down at himself and saw his pants ripped open like his legs had exploded through them. His shirt hung in taters and his feet were bare. He may as well have been running around naked.

The cops were clearly there for him, of that there was no question. An officer pointed a six-shooter at him and called out, "What have you done with Phil Baxter? We know that's his truck."

At that, Phil ran, leaped over a cruiser and was into the woods quicker than even he thought was possible. Shots rang out after him, one clipped his right thigh, but he just kept on running.

He ran for what felt like half an hour before he decided to take a breath. The woods were dark and scary. He was sweating and the cold air was starting to give him a chill. He didn't think of himself as an outdoorsman, but he was no city slicker either. He knew sweat and cold air was a bad combination. He checked the spot where the bullet had grazed him. The pant leg had been further ripped by the bullet, but his skin showed no sign of injury. And yet he had felt the bite of the slug as it had cut into him.

Phil couldn't tell what direction he was heading in the dark. He had no resources. Spending the night in the woods seemed like a forgone conclusion. He set about collecting anything that might keep him warm overnight. The only thing he could scrounge up where a pile of leaves. He piled them high and squirmed his way into them. Exhaustion brought about sleep almost instantly.

The sun rose over a misty forest and the squirrels and scavengers were busy hunting and hiding food. Phil squinted at the daylight, sitting up and taking in his surroundings. He'd grown again, but not as much as the days before.

His stomach ached. Hunger pangs racked his body. This must be what it feels like to be an addict. To lose control over your will power. To have one thing take center stage in your life. He was very cold, his muscles were stiff, but the need for food drowned out all other signals.

He got to his feet and went in search of sustenance; the sound of a helicopter filled the sky above.

He walked for hours; the hunger increased with each step until it reached a fever point. He crashed out of the woods and found himself in an open expanse with a large factory at the far end. A saccharine scent floated from the building and drew in Phil like a paid lover. He ran towards the factory breaking through a chain linked fence and shoving a few parked cars out of his way. The building was covered with corrugated panels, which proved easy to peal away. Phil made himself his own entry way tearing the sheet metal apart like it was foil.

Once inside terrified workers abandoned their posts and ran in all directions. A man driving a forklift jumped off while the forklift continued unmanned, crashing into Phil. Phil barely noticed it, but he did notice a large container of newly minted chocolates that the forklift had been ferrying. He stuck a hand into the container and withdrew a massive caloric goldmine. He stuffed his face, handful after handful, a melted chocolate ring forming around his face.

He ate most of the container, before he spied chocolate cherry cordials. He loved cherries. He gorged on them until he noticed they had just about every type of nut in large bins. He ate all the cashews first, then the pistachios. By the time he'd finished those he was feeling satiated and was a little disappointed to hear police sirens in the distance.

He would have preferred to nap but decided to make a run

for the woods. He had a good idea of where he was now and thought he could find himself a safe place to take a snooze.

PHIL WOKE inside an old barn that belonged to a meat packing factory. They had once raised the cows here on the land but found it more profitable to move into the cutting and shipping side of things. The barn sat unused.

Phil stood and the top of his head burst through the barn roof. Old hay went flying and he disturbed a nesting pair of birds. The absurdity of his current situation was not evident to him though. The hunger pangs were back and in full force. His large olfactory senses could smell the beef, pork and other delicacies waiting within the building.

He walked through the barn dragging it behind him like a bath towel for a few steps before the building collapsed behind him. The walls of the meat packing plant were solid concrete. Phil decided to rip off the roof like he was opening a can of beans.

Inside workers ran for their lives while Phil pawed at the bins and ate meat like it was small pieces of beef jerky. This was perhaps the best meal he'd had in days.

The police arrived quickly this time. Two helicopters circled overhead and a S.W.A.T. team deployed themselves into key positions. Phil paid them no more attention than he would a fly at a picnic. Annoying but no real threat.

It seemed the authorities planned to change Phil's mind on that subject. They immediately opened fire on him with everything they had. Snipers fired from helicopters, machine guns were fired by the S.W.A.T. teams and Phil continued to eat, occasionally swatting away an officer or vehicle like he would a mosquito.

By the time he'd finished with the meat packers there were no more mosquitoes to squash.

PHIL HAD EATEN his way south, destroying entire ecosystems as he went. He'd drained more than one lake to quench his thirst. The army had been called in to put him down, but he'd grown so large, and his body healed so quicky now that there wasn't much in their arsenal that could really hurt him.

With his large size he could cross vast distances quickly. It was inevitable that he would eventually find himself in a large city. There were plenty of resources to be had there and his consumption of those resources was immense.

At five AM on December Twenty-third, Phil entered the metropolis of Toronto. Many had already evacuated the city, but a large number stayed to film him for their social media empires, figuring the footage was worth the risk.

Phil had gorged himself on the trip to the city. He now stood approximately 2000 feet tall. He stood in the downtown core beside the CN Tower, his left hand resting on the top spire. He was looking out over Lake Ontario, wondering if he might enjoy a swim.

The Canadian government had reached out to their southern neighbours requested military aid. Their neighbours were more than happy to oblige. They sent enough aircraft, drones, submarines, and troops to quash World War III. Unfortunately, the military complex that supplied all these weapons had never designed them for warfare against a giant man who healed almost instantly.

They constantly brought up the 'N' word. The UN council and the Canadian Government always replied negative to nuclear arms, but their resistance was dwindling.

Phil felt a queasy feeling in his stomach. He'd come across a feed silo yesterday and all the fiber was playing havoc with his innards. He spied the sports center that usually housed a Toronto baseball team. With its retractable roof open it was reminiscent of something he hadn't been able to use in some time. He sat himself down on the stadium and evacuated his bowels. Toronto had just become a bio contaminated nightmare.

Phil bathed in the Lake, then ate all the city had to offer.

By Christmas he was so large that he had to crouch to avoid his head leaving the protective layer of Earth's atmosphere. He'd freeze-dried his hair a few times accidentally. The desire to consume only increased with his size. He only had fleeting moments of his own thoughts. In those precious times he thought of Martha and the kids.

On Boxing Day, the neighbours to the south got the go ahead. Nuclear arms were cleared to be dropped on the city of Toronto. Two Northrop Grumman B-2 Spirit Bombers, also known as stealth bombers, lifted off from the Niagara Falls Air Reserve Station crossed the border into Canadian airspace and approached the target from Lake Ontario.

The planes released their packages flawlessly. Two guided bombs landed either side of a crouched Phil Baxter and detonated a combined destructive power of 2.4 megatons. One hundred and twenty times the power of the bombs dropped on Nagasaki in 1945.

Phil felt the stabbing pain that those bombs produced. He felt like he'd been stabbed by shards of glass. His reaction was immediate. He stood up.

His head and shoulders breached into the cold of space. At his feet he was feeling the temperatures of two nuclear blasts. At his head he was feeling the bite of minus four-hundred-and fifty-three-degrees Fahrenheit. Frost was forming on his face and chest. His feet were blistering. His body healed him as quicky as it could, but even his great constitution could not keep up with the relentless cold of outer space.

His head froze solid, and Phil's body tipped backwards as he fell back to earth.

————————

ALSO FLOATING in outer space was a circular shaped craft. On board two beings watched as Phil was torched and iced at the same time. They displayed joy as his corpse fell back to the planet. They had anticipated this as an outcome but hadn't dared hoped that this scenario would play itself out.

A billion years ago humans had become problematic. A massive space rock was hurled towards their planet reaching about Forty-three thousand miles per hour. The impact had occurred in what the humans called Sudbury.

Destroying a species was an artistic pursuit. There were many beautiful symmetries to the rock impacting Sudbury, Ontario and the being Phil impacting Toronto, Ontario. On a planetary scale, it's almost the same spot.

And just like the impact a billion years ago, Phil's impact would create massive shock waves, tsunamis, and a nuclear winter caused by a massive ash cloud.

The two beings embraced one another.

Small ships similar to their own began to exit subspace with grand flashes of light. The others were coming to witness the event. It would be the most discussed event of their culture.

They would talk about the artistry, the nod to history and the moral implications. Humans had died from greed, overeating and all their base inclinations. This moment would be reinterpreted by all their people's artists.

The two beings would accept the accolades and enjoy the moment, but already they were thinking about the next planet. The next event.

Art is a calling one must answer.

And you're only as good as your last omnicide.

GOT STEAMPUNK MAGIC?

NINA KIRIKI HOFFMAN

Acclaimed veteran fantasy writer Nina Kiriki Hoffman is known for writing fantastically fun fantasy, and some amazingly dark stories that will twist you up. This is one of those darker stories, but don't worry, you are in the hands of a master and she will keep you safe.

Nina is a musician, a writing instructor, and a judge for Writers of the Future.

And she is amazingly fun to be around if you get the chance.

THE WHOLE OF THE WIDENESS OF NIGHT

NINA KIRIKI HOFFMAN

I lay in bed with my eyes shut, listening. My head was still full of nightmares, giant rabid rats like the ones my brother Chris told me about last night right before Dad sent us to bed. Red-eyed rats with disease-drool bubbling out of their mouths, chasing me down dirty alleys where trash tripped me and slime coated my hands and knees every time I fell. Chittering noises and the scrabble of claws, the smell of sewers, always coming closer no matter how fast I ran.

The dream's terror still gripped me even though I was awake. I tried to calm down enough to hear something besides my heart.

All I heard was my own room. The clock hummed. Nothing else. No rat chitters, no claws on the floor, no dark city noises. No older brothers breathing.

I sniffed. No really disgusting scents — decaying dead bodies, puke, Brussels sprouts.

I reached under my pillow and found my lizard stone. It fitted perfectly into my hand. I held it and opened my eyes.

I screamed.

A skull lay facing me on the pillow, white bone, white teeth, shadowed cheekbones, black nose holes, eye sockets. Except, in the middle of the eye sockets, bright green eyes; and ratty brown hair on top of the head. I screamed and screamed and screamed, even after I realized this was my very own baby doll, Patty, painted to look like a skull.

How could they do that? I stopped for breath. My throat hurt. I picked up Patty and touched her face. Painted on — with acrylic paints, the kind that didn't come off. Skull-face Patty. She'd be like that the rest of her life. I hugged her to my stomach, my right hand still closed on the lizard stone. My favorite doll, the one Daddy gave me when I was five, the one I slept with every Christmas Eve. How could they?

My bedroom door opened and all three of my brothers looked in. "Gooooood morning," Ray said. They grinned, looking like sloppy copies of each other: shaggy dark hair, narrow blue eyes, and wide mouths, especially when stretched into mean smiles. At fourteen, Ray was oldest. Will was thirteen, and Chris was eleven and a half.

I felt sick to my stomach. Probably Ray planned this. Will was the artist — I bet he did the actual painting. Chris, the best sneak, most likely put Patty on my bed.

"Get out of my room," I said. My throat was sore from screaming.

"We couldn't help it," Ray said, still smiling. "You have the best scream in the world."

"Get out! And close the door!" I wanted to throw something at them, but the only things in reach were Patty and my lizard stone.

"Come on, Lizzie, don't be like that. It was really funny!" said Ray. Will had lost his smile, though. Chris turned and left. Finally Ray got the message too. He slammed the door.

I studied Patty. I spat on my finger and wiped it on her white cheek. No, this wasn't the kind of paint that came off.

I did cry a little while I was getting dressed for school. I put Patty on the dresser by the play makeup kit Mom had given me for my tenth birthday a couple weeks past, and the little gold unicorn Grandma gave me last Christmas. Patty still looked scary, but if I stared really hard I could see her smiling friendly face under all that paint.

How could they?

Easy. They did stuff like this all the time.

At least it was daytime now, and night was hours away. During the day I did all right. As long as I could see things clearly, I could get over being scared. It was at night, when I woke up with nightmares in my head and couldn't look around and be sure they weren't true, that was the worst.

Sometimes night went on forever.

I looked at my lizard stone. It was a brown stone with a lizard painted on it in black ink. My aunt Elizabeth, my dad's sister whom I was named after, gave it to me for my eighth birthday. She said she knew what it was like to be the only girl in a family of boys. She said Indians painted the lizard, and it had secret powers to protect me. I wasn't sure I liked it at first. Ray and Chris called me "Lizard" when they wanted to be mean. But I liked the stone more and more as time went on. I took it everywhere with me. Even when I was scared, I could hold the lizard stone and find calm. I started getting other lizard things after that.

I stuffed my notebook and a couple of textbooks into my iridescent lizard-skin backpack and added tights, my toe shoes, and a leotard. Mom was supposed to take me to my ballet class after school. Half the time she forgot. Sometimes I got a ride with my friend Galina's mom. I practiced ballet moves every day at a barre Dad had put up in the basement, but it was hard to improve when I didn't get to class half the time.

The recital was coming up. I had a really neat outfit for the big corps de ballet number, but with all my misses, I wasn't even sure Madame Inessa would let me be in the dance.

I opened the bedroom door and jumped and screamed. A big black construction paper spider with red jellybean eyes dangled from a thread right where it could hit me in the face. Before I really saw it, I thought it was covered with fur and had glowing eyes. My heart thumped hard and fast. When I could see straight, I tore the spider down and ripped it up. If I didn't, they could use it again, and for sure it would scare me again. No matter how many times I told myself to ignore all the stuff my brothers put me through, they scored a scare off me every time. I was so totally sick and tired of it.

I heard Chris laughing down the hall. My stomach started grinding.

"Kids! Breakfast! Eat it now or it goes in the garbage!" Dad yelled.

I stomped down the hall and then down the stairs, anger heating me all through. Why was I afraid of every stupid little thing? If only I could stop screaming!

I went to the counter and grabbed the lunch bag with my name on it and stuffed it into my backpack before I sat down at the table. If I didn't, some brother would steal all the good stuff. "Hi, sweetie," Mom said to me, plopping a plate with two runny fried eggs on it in front of me. I can't stand runny eggs. I don't mind wet yolks, but I hate wet whites. She gave me two pieces of dry toast, something else I wasn't fond of, but she was always putting me on a diet, and then telling my brothers to eat eat eat and grow big and strong. I spread the egg yolks on the toast and ate that.

Luckily Dad was reading the newspaper. Maybe he wouldn't notice I was wasting the whites.

I was just about to slip the egg whites down the garbage disposal when Will said, "Hey, Dad, is Lizzie supposed to be doing that?"

"What are you doing, Lizzie?" Dad asked, looking up from the paper.

"Nothing." I stared at the runny whites on my plate. I felt sick to my stomach. I couldn't stand the thought of that stuff coating my tongue. I would throw up for sure. I looked up at Mom, and she looked scared, so I shoved the egg whites into my mouth and tried to swallow them before I could feel them, but I gagged instead.

I ran to the downstairs bathroom and coughed them back up, along with the rest of my breakfast. My mouth tasted like acid.

"Lizzie! Bus!" Dad yelled. "Be on it now or be grounded for the weekend!"

I washed out my mouth, then ran for the bus. We were

going to the carnival tomorrow. No way did I want to miss that.

Chris and I went to the same school. Will and Ray were in middle school and caught a different bus. I raced up the steps onto the bus right behind Chris and prayed with all the lizard power I had that I could find a seat next to somebody else, even Pinchmaster George. Chris and I were almost the last kids the driver picked up, and sometimes we had no choice of seats.

I found a seat next to Galina. She always tried to save me one, but sometimes she couldn't. Chris sat way in the back with some other skater boys.

I hadn't managed to finish much of my homework. I got so sleepy after dinner, but then I never got any real sleep because of the nightmares. I felt really stupid in class. Nothing new about that.

At first recess I was checking my lunch for something small and edible to replace the breakfast I hadn't managed to hang onto when this guy from sixth grade, Oscar, caught me, knocked me down, and took my lunch away. This was around a corner where no teachers were.

But Chris saw it, and he rushed up and kicked Oscar down and got my lunch back for me. He grabbed my arm and dragged me around the building to a safer place in case Oscar got to his feet again — Oscar was half a head taller than Chris.

For once in my life I was happy to see my brother. "Wow, thanks," I said.

Chris smiled. "Us Wakefields got to stick together," he said. Then he went through my lunch himself. He took my cherry pie and my banana, but he left me carrots, a bologna sandwich, and a juice box.

Pretty good, considering.

I ate the carrots.

———————

I WISHED Mom would let me put a lock on my door. A padlock, anything. But she wouldn't.

When I opened my closet to put my school clothes away after school (and another missed ballet class), this dusty white thing dropped down over my head and tangled me up. I screamed and screamed, trying to fight loose, but I was enveloped in cool, white, webby, ghostly stuff. Panic stung me and stung me while I thrashed around, screaming. I couldn't think.

After I tired myself out, I managed to wriggle loose and found out it wasn't anything but an old torn sheet with fake Halloween cobwebby stuff on it, sprayed with Pam or some nonstick stuff so it was slippery and clammy.

I just broke down and cried for a while. I was too tired not to. I had thought a ghost swallowed me whole and I was stuck in its stomach forever.

Why did they do this? Which brother set this one up? How could I make them stop?

Complaining to Mom did no good. She said it wasn't ladylike to scream so much. Dad said he hated a snitch, and boys would be boys. People always said that. Was it ever not true? When was a boy not a boy? How did you get that to happen?

I ripped up the sheet and stomped on it. Dad yelled through the floor for me not to make such a racket. For a couple minutes I jumped up and down even harder, wishing I could stomp a hole right through the floor and fall through to my death. Wouldn't that show everybody a thing or two? Yeah, I'd break both arms and legs and stove in my ribs so the bones stuck up from the shattered, bloody flesh. Blood would bubble from my mouth as I gurgled my last. They'd be sorry then.

"LIZZIE, STOP THAT JUMPING NOW OR YOU ARE CONFINED TO YOUR ROOM FOR THE REST OF THE MONTH," Dad screamed.

Oh, man, oh, wait a minute. The carnival was tomorrow! I stopped jumping. I had to stop misbehaving at least long enough to get to the carnival. Last year they had had these really neat stuffed lizards at the concession booth, but I had used all my allowance on rides before I saw the lizards. This year I was going to buy a lizard first. Who needed rides? My whole life was one big carnival ride.

I shoved the shreds of ghost sheet under my bed and lay

down. I was so tired I slept through dinner, but Ray came and woke me up in time to do the dishes.

I HAD ASKED Mom to hold onto my allowance for two weeks. It was no use my trying to save any money myself. No matter where I hid it in my room, somebody else in the house found it and stole it, unless I spent it as soon as I got it.

I tried to get her to bring her purse into the living room when she gave me the money so Ray and Will and Chris wouldn't see, but, as always, she was oblivious to hints. "Here you are, darling," she said right there in the kitchen at the breakfast table. She handed me two five-dollar bills. "Have a wonderful time." She gave me another six dollars for the entry fee, and handed money around to my brothers too.

"Are you sure you don't want to come, Mom?" I asked. "I know you like the merry-go-round." She had a little collection of porcelain carousel horses. She'd been so upset when Ray broke her favorite.

If only she'd come to the fair with us, maybe the boys would leave me alone for two minutes.

"I'm too old for things like that," she said. She smiled at me. Was she too old? I stared into her face. I saw tiny lines at the edges of her mouth and the corners of her eyes, and deep down I saw some kind of heavy tired that made me wonder how she even got up in the morning. "Just go. Go, and have a wonderful time." She kissed my cheek. Her lips felt as cold as the gravestones in last night's dream.

Oh yeah. Last night's dream. Running through an endless

graveyard to get away from vampire ghosts, tripping over gravestones, falling into graves. Chris had told me a nice story about spirit-sucking ghosts last night right before I went to sleep .

I clutched my lizard stone in my pocket and made the graveyard go away.

The fairgrounds were at the edge of town, next door to the old school that burned down in the thirties. We took the bus. I waited for Ray, Will, and Chris to get off ahead of me, hoping they'd rush off and leave me alone, but Ray made them stay. "We're supposed to look after you," he said.

Yeah, right.

We paid our way into the carnival. I headed right to the concession booths, picked out my lizard — a really great turquoise one with a green tail, and he only cost seven dollars! — and reached into my pocket.

No money.

I looked back. My brothers stood there watching me with grins on their faces. Chris held up two five-dollar bills and rubbed them against each other. He had been practicing pick-pocket skills. They all laughed when they saw how mad I was.

I checked my other pocket for the lizard stone. Whew! It was still there.

I raced to Chris and tried to get the money away from him, but he passed it to Will, and Will passed it to Ray.

"Come on. That's my money," I said. "Give it back!"

"We're older. We're smarter. We know how to use money better than you do," Ray said.

"I waited all year for this." I looked over my shoulder at the perfect lizard, which the concession guy had already put back on the shelf. "Come on. Give it back."

Will lost his smile. He looked at Ray. Chris did too, his head cocked. Ray put on a thoughtful expression. For about thirty seconds I thought he might cave, but then he said, "Nawww. We'll show you how to have some real fun."

They bought long strips of tickets, and they took me on the Haunted House ride. Which I went on because I figured it was probably the only thing I was going to get to do at the carnival. There were some neat things in it, like a huge Frankenstein with glowing eyes, and mirrors that made us look totally twisted, and glow-in-the-dark ghosts, and a horde of chittering bats that dropped from the ceiling and flapped around our heads, but even though the production was much more professional than all the things my brothers thought up, the ride wasn't half as scary as life at home. I mean, on the ride, I knew in advance I was supposed to get scared. Which wasn't what I usually thought when I opened my closet door. Though by this time....

Anyway, I guess I didn't scream enough to satisfy Ray. He was bummed by the end of the ride.

After that, my brothers went on the octopus and the hammer and the Tilt-a-whirl, and they didn't take me.

So I watched: I watched gleaming carnival machinery spin people around and throw them up and drop them down, with a soundtrack of screams. I watched people shoot things and throw things and toss things and lose things, and every once in a while somebody won something. A kid won a bowl with a goldfish in it by tossing a ping-pong ball. An old lady won a green glass dish by landing a dime in it. A boy threw fifteen darts and popped fifteen balloons and gave his girlfriend a big stuffed dog. I watched people eat fair food: pink, green, and blue cotton candy, corn dogs, elephant ear pastries, sno-cones. I smelled all those good carnival smells, popcorn, peanuts, animals, people, and dust.

My brothers whooped as they came off the Viking Ship ride, and ran on sneakered feet toward the next ride. Will stopped, though, and came back. "Here," he whispered, and handed me four tickets and a dollar. "I'm sorry."

"Whatcha doin', Will?" Ray yelled. Will turned and ran after him.

Four tickets and a dollar. I could pick a ride. If it was something stupid, I might even have a ticket left over. There wasn't much I could do with a dollar. Most of the snacks were at least a dollar twenty-five. Still, it was better than nothing.

I stood up and shoved my treasure in my pocket, then wandered around looking at everything. Now that I thought I might be able to do something, it all looked completely different. The colors were sharper and the smells smelled even better. "Maybe" sang in my brain.

Still, it wasn't enough to buy the perfect lizard, even if I turned my tickets in or sold them to somebody else.

I checked out each of the rides. Some took five tickets, but a lot took four. Bumper cars? The merry-go-round? One of the little roller coasters? The Tilt-a-whirl?

I walked past the Haunted House ride and noticed a small dark booth for the first time. It was like a tent, but the red canvas roof had corner poles that curled up like the roofs of Chinese buildings in movies, and there was no open side; the whole thing was curtained in black. A small yellow sign hung in front. In red print, it said, "Fondest Dreams. Largest Hopes. Best Wishes. Madama Syzygy." Below that, in smaller print, "Fortunes. Potions. Curses."

There was nothing about how many tickets it would take.

Fortune-telling always gave me the creeps. I mean, so you found out what to expect. What were you supposed to do about it? I'd rather be surprised. If I knew what to expect, I would probably find out it was all going to be the same for the rest of my life: my stupid brothers, scaring me every time I turned around because they liked to hear me scream. Maybe four years in the future, Ray would go away to college, but Will and Chris would still be around. Even four more years of scares felt endless to me.

I wondered if there was a potion that would make boys stop being boys. If there was, I probably couldn't afford it.

I went away and watched people throw darts and dimes, squirt water guns and pitch baseballs. Will and Ray and Chris went past, munching hot dogs. I stayed in the shadow of other people and they didn't see me. They looked so happy. Sure. It was easy for them. What did they have to be scared of?

I walked up one aisle and down the next, studying each of the rides, all of the pitch games, every snack and concession stand. I didn't see a single ride I really wanted to go on. My stomach grumbled, but none of the food smelled good to me anymore. The only thing I craved with all my heart was the turquoise lizard with the green tail. And I wasn't going to get that. Even if my brothers had a change of heart, they wouldn't have any money left by now.

When had they ever had a change of heart?

I found myself in front of Madama Syzygy's tent again. "Hello?" I said.

The curtain parted in the middle. One side drew back. A pale face peered at me from under a mountain of bright red hair. "Hello," she said in a deep, pleasant voice. "Won't you come in?"

"How much does it cost?"

"Coming in is free. We will negotiate anything further."

I came in.

It smelled like spicy incense. A small table stood between two chairs. Black curtains hung all around, but it wasn't dark inside; two bowls of light sat on the table. I'd never seen anything like that before. I wanted to check them out, but I glanced at Madama Syzygy first to see if it was okay.

Her clothes blazed with a thousand winking lights as she moved. I looked harder and saw she wore a flowing black dress with little round mirrors sewn all over it. "Please be seated," she said. She drifted around behind the table and sat in that chair herself. It was a fancy one, like a throne, carved from black wood. The arms had dragons on them. Her hands rested on the dragons' heads, right above their pale, bone-white eyes.

The chair I sat in was one of those metal folding ones, with a fancy tufted cushion on it. When I sat, my knees slid under the edge of the silky tablecloth. I got a lapful of fringe. I glanced at one of the light bowls and still couldn't figure it out. It looked like a plain glass bowl full of glowing white water. Maybe neon worked like that.

"What can I do for you?" she asked.

"I don't know," I said. Suddenly I felt like crying. I hauled out the four sweaty tickets and the dollar bill Will had given me and dropped them on the table. "This is all I've got."

She stared at them for a moment, then touched them. "And what do you want in return?"

"I don't know," I whispered. I didn't want my fortune told. Either it was all lies, or it was going to be bad.

"What is your heart's fondest wish?" she murmured.

"A blue lizard with a green tail."

She laughed. After a second I laughed too. She had that kind of laugh. And then she said, in this low, compelling voice like the one I sometimes heard in dreams, "What is the wish under that wish?"

"I want to scare my brothers worse than they ever scared me," I whispered, without even thinking about it. "I want to scare them so bad they'll never sleep at night again. That's what I want."

I sat up straight. No way. No way would I ever think that, let alone say it out loud to a stranger.

Her dark eyes sparkled. She smiled at me. "Now, that is a worthy wish," she said.

"It's not really what I want." I looked away from her.

"Isn't it?"

I thought. Wouldn't it be great, though? To scare my brothers right out of their socks? Wouldn't that be the best thing in the world? So they would know what it felt like. Once they knew, maybe they'd stop.

"I'd like it," I whispered.

"Let's negotiate."

"You can't give me such a great wish for only a dollar and some tickets."

"No," she said. "I accept other forms of payment, though."

"I don't have anything else."

"What's in your other pocket?"

I reached into my pocket and found my lizard stone.

Not my lizard stone. My comfort in the middle of nightmares. My secret power name. My breath when my throat tightened so much I thought I'd die.

"For that," she said, "I can give your brothers a scare they will never get over."

I held my lizard stone in my hand for a long time. What would it be like, next time they scared me, not to have my lizard stone? I could always find another rock, but it wouldn't have the shape and the texture that this one did. It wouldn't have the black lizard painted on it, the secret power inside. It wouldn't be able to protect me the way this one did.

If I scared my brothers so bad they couldn't get over it, maybe they'd get out of the scare business and I wouldn't need the lizard stone anymore.

It would be worth it.

Slowly I set the lizard stone on the table. It was hard to make my fingers let go of it.

———————

I snuck into the bathroom at midnight after everyone else had gone to sleep. I couldn't run the bathtub taps full blast without making too much noise, so I kept the hot water down to a trickle. I poured the powder from the packet Madama Syzygy had given me under the running water and watched as it turned the water milk white. A strange swampy smell came from it. At first I thought it was awful, but then I started to like it. I almost wanted to drink it.

What if it was poison? What if it was all fake? Why did I ever trust that woman? I must have been crazy.

I sat on the floor by the bathtub waiting for it to get full enough for me to lie in, and thought about the bedtime story Chris had told me tonight. Dreamseeds, he called it.

Strange plants from outer space landed and grew in all the parks in all the cities in all the world. They bloomed at night and sent out spores. Dreamseeds. The spores drifted around until they found open windows in houses, and then they went inside where people were sleeping, and they slipped into their ears and planted themselves in their brains. Their roots sucked on peoples' brain juices and their flowers gave people nightmares all night, every night, and after they'd lived in your head a while they started giving you nightmares during the day. You'd think you were awake, but you'd start seeing ghosts and dead bodies every time you turned around, and at last, nothing could wake you up from it.

Sure, you could close the window, Chris told me, but sometimes the spores snuck into the house through a door — and he opened the front door to the night — and then floated around in a house until everybody fell asleep. They like young minds the best, Chris said.

But I wasn't asleep right now, and Chris was. His was the youngest sleeping mind in the house now.

The tub filled slowly. The water stayed pure white. How did it do that when there was so much more water now? Maybe the magic was real.

I looked at the counter where I had put my outfit for tonight. It was the beautiful dress I had for the ballet recital I'd never be in, and my toe shoes, and the wreath of silk flowers for my hair. Beside it sat the other thing Madama Syzygy had given me, a magic wand with a jester's head on top. "Tap their foreheads with this to wake them," she had told me. "It will help them be ready for fear."

It gave me the creeps, for sure. The jester had a skull's face.

Dreamseeds. Maybe Chris had one of those dreamseeds in his head. Otherwise how did he come up with these nightmare stories for me every night?

After tonight...I would plant a seed myself.

The water was high enough in the tub to cover me now. I turned off the tap and looked at the water, which steamed gently and smelled like wet pulled weeds on a hot day.

I heard a news story on the radio the other day about a kid who lived where the water was bad and got leukemia. A lot of other kids in his neighborhood got it too. Cancer clusters. There was another nightmare. What if this stuff was that kind of poison? Real poison?

I thought of nightmares every night, of ghosts in my closet, spiders in my doorway, slugs in my lunch bag, waking up to find my hands and feet tied together so I couldn't move. I thought of my doll's new paint job. What would they think of next?

I took off my nightgown and slipped into the bathtub.

The water felt warm and thick against my skin, slick and slimy like mud. It was really an awful feeling at first, but then I liked it. I sat down in it, then lay down. Finally I closed my eyes and put my head right under, the way Madama Syzygy had instructed me, and held my breath as long as I could. I felt like I was floating in something soft and warm. I couldn't hear even the normal underwater noises. I heard nothing.

I didn't want to sit up. I could stay like this forever, safe in the warm white nothing. Yep. This was all right.

Then I ran out of breath. I sat up and rubbed my eyes.

My hands and my face felt weird. Way too bony.

I didn't want to open my eyes.

Something slithered down my back.

Without opening my eyes, I reached for the plug and pulled it. I sat while the swampy water drained from around me. It took the warmth with it, until I was freezing and trembling and chattering. Then I had to open my eyes, even if I got some of that white water in them. Chattering? Not just my teeth, but my feet, my elbows, my rear against the tub, a storm of clicks and clacks.

I opened my eyes a slit and stared down at myself. Most of me was gone. Only my skeleton was left. My hair clogged the drain. All of it had fallen out.

I screamed once. The sound that came out of my mouth scared me. It was all hollow and echoey.

I gripped the side of the tub with my skeletal hands and pulled myself up on the bones of my feet. I felt so cold. And then, suddenly, that went away and I didn't feel much of anything.

It had to be some kind of trick.

I looked down at my chest and saw only a rib cage with nothing inside. I poked my bony finger at my chest and it went right between the ribs and wriggled around inside me.

Maybe this was just another dream.

I ran the shower then, not caring if I had the water on full blast. I sort of hoped Mom or Dad or somebody would come to the bathroom and wake me up. This had to be a dream.

The last of the white water ran off me, though, and I stayed bony. I picked up the hair in the drain and my skeletal fingers got all tangled in it. I managed to flip it off my hand and into the wastebasket under the sink, but it wasn't easy.

I saw myself in the mirror and had to scream again. My head was just a skull! I couldn't see my eyes! What was I looking with? I watched the skull's lower jaw flap open as I screamed, showing a mouthful of nothing. No way!

How could I move? How could I think? How could I even scream, if all I was was bones? How could Madama Syzygy do this to me?

I pinched myself. It didn't help. I could hear it click, but I couldn't feel it.

I stared at my image until I got tired of doing that. Okay. I was like this now. Or this was a weird dream. Either way, I had better things to do than stand here staring.

I used a towel, but it was scary drying myself off. I kept reaching into parts of myself I could never touch before.

I dressed in my ballet outfit. Nothing fit anymore, but I got it to stay on. I had to tie my toe shoes on really tight and knot the ribbons between my bones to hold them up. My flower wreath, though, settled onto my skull and sat there just fine.

Somehow I looked better dressed. There was less naked bone.

Finally I picked up the jester wand. The bells on his cap jingled. Strange strength flowed into me. His little skull-face looked up at me and said, "Hi, beautiful. Let's go out and terrorize."

Suddenly that was all I wanted to do.

First I went to Ray's room. What a pit. I wondered if he

ever picked anything up. There were dirty clothes every-where, books dropped here and there, sports equipment and comics scattered across the floor. I tripped on a basketball on my way across the room, but Ray never stirred.

Look how he slept, with a smile on his face, breathing easy, no fears. I watched him sleep for a long time.

"Time's a-wasting, beautiful," the jester said.

I shook myself, — clack, clack — leaned over, and tapped Ray's forehead with the jester. "Ray," I murmured. My voice came out hollow and spooky. "Oh, Ray. Wake up."

He sighed in his sleep, turned over, and opened his eyes.

Then he screamed.

It was the most beautiful sound I had ever heard. He screamed really loud, and for a long, long time. He backed away from me until he bumped into the wall behind his bed, and he kept shoving with his feet even though he couldn't go any farther. I didn't even have to do anything. He screamed and screamed.

The light flicked on. I turned to look and saw Chris and Will standing in the doorway, staring. Then they started screaming too, and clutching each other.

So sweet. Life was great!

"It's a...it's a...," Ray stammered when they'd all run out of air. "It's got to be a trick." His voice cracked in the middle of the sentence.

I rose to my toes and did three pirouettes, my arms outstretched.

Will and Chris were panting. "It's got to be a dream," Chris said.

"That's right. Just a dream," said Ray.

I danced over and pinched his cheek with my fingerbones. He screamed and collapsed again. Two tours jetés and I reached the door. I patted Will on the cheek, and then I, well, I grabbed Chris's head and kissed him right on the mouth to thank him for all those nighttime stories I hadn't been able to stop myself from listening to. Will shrieked and staggered backward. Chris collapsed to the floor as soon as I let go of him. I slipped out into the hall and toe-stepped to the top of the stairs, where I turned and waved the jester at them. The jester laughed maniacally. I started down.

"What's all that damned racket up there?" yelled Dad, stepping to the foot of the stairs. "You kids are noisy every night, but this is worse than usual — ai-yi-yiiiieee!"

I tapped his shoulder with the jester wand and he backed away from me, leaving me a clear path to the front door. I went out.

"Wait."

I stopped on the porch and looked back. Mom stood in the doorway, her hair up in curlers, her robe tight around her. "What are you doing in Lizzie's ballet costume? Who are you?"

"Mom?" I whispered.

She came out onto the porch in her bare feet. "Lizzie? Is that a costume? What are you doing?"

"Scaring my brothers."

"But..." She touched my cheekbone. "Lizzie! What happened to you? Lizzie — "

I ran.

I stopped at a bus stop shelter three blocks away. I sat on the bench and fluffed my skirts out, then thought back over the last half hour. The best night of my life. Finally I got to be the monster, and now I didn't have to be afraid of anything. Ray, screaming. What a great scared face! Chris collapsing, almost fainting. Just because of me! Will backing away. Just because of a few bones. They'd never be able to tease me about being scared again. Just let them try it.

I smiled and smiled. At least, I felt like I was smiling.

"So when does this wear off?" I asked the jester wand at last.

"Wear off?" he said.

"When do I go back to being my flesh-and-blood self?"

"You don't."

"What?"

"You got what you paid for. A scare they'll never get over. We can do it again tomorrow night, and every night if you want! Isn't it great?"

———

No BUSES RAN this late at night, and I wasn't sure if any driver would have let me on anyway. I ended up walking back to the fairgrounds. It didn't matter. I didn't get tired.

But I was too late. Madama Syzygy's booth wasn't there anymore. The rides and pitch booths and snack stands were gone. Nothing was left but a litter of candy wrappers, a few squashed cans, and a big black Ferris wheel. I heard fractured music and creaking noises from the wheel. It was running, even this late at night.

Maybe the people running the Ferris wheel would know where Madama Syzygy had gone. Maybe they wouldn't run screaming when they saw me; maybe they'd wait long enough for me to ask questions. Maybe they saw people like me all the time.

I walked through the night toward the wheel. I wondered if day would ever come.

LISA SILVERTHORNE

Acclaimed veteran fantasy and science fiction writer Lisa Silverthorne makes a setting come alive in this story like no other writer can. In fact, just glance at the first sentence of this story. Maybe one of the best first sentences I have seen as an editor. Amazing.

Lisa sells her fantastic short fiction to many, many markets, including just this last holiday a couple stories to the Holiday Spectacular.

For a lot more about Lisa's stories and her growing new Game of Lost Souls series, and other new fantasy series, plus the beautiful covers she designs, go to http://www.lisasilverthorne.com/

WHEN SPARROWS FALL

LISA SILVERTHORNE

It begins with a chill wind and screams. Burnt scent of jet fuel and whistle of air across torn wings. I toss in my bed, desperately wanting it to be a dream, and flail against the terrified voices, the hush of descent. There is a horrible, rushing sound in my ears. At the whisper of death and the gouging of metal against ground, I bolt up from the bed, my skin clammy with sweat. My stomach aches and tears gather in my eyes. *Please – not another one.*

Turning on the light, I sit up and hug my pillow. Icy fear trembles through my body and my teeth chatter. I rock against the headboard, trying to dislodge the images. My hands hurt. I glance down at them. They're burnt and smell of jet fuel. My hands haven't burned in a long time. It's a bad crash – a jet. Lots of people.

Sunrise is a couple of hours off and he'll be calling. Maybe by then I can pull myself together?

In a short while, my shaking stops, the blankets at last

warming me. I rise slowly and go into the kitchen to make some coffee. After two cups, I slip into the shower and dress. The horizon is fiery now. I pour myself another cup of coffee and wait.

Finally, I lay my hand against the phone and a heartbeat later, it rings. My trembling returns.

"Hello, Mark," I say, my voice raspy.

"Uh – Stacia?" NTSB Investigator Mark Vincent's voice shakes more than usual this time.

"It's a jet, isn't it?" I ask, my hands still throbbing.

A long sigh hisses through the receiver. "Yes, Stace. Two hundred people dead. Only one survivor. We're still looking for the black box."

My heart twists at the ghostly feel of a stuffed bear and the image of a little girl clutching it like a life preserver, her head down. The whistle of air across the plane's fuselage echoes in the phone's static. The impact is sharp then numbing. I lurch forward. The silence is heavy. They always call me when the black box is lost.

I glance out the window at the darkness beginning to lighten on the horizon and I hear the fragile chirp of birds. Morning will come soon.

They say that God hears even a sparrow when it falls to the ground. What must He hear when two hundred of his own fall?

"I'll be there in four hours," I say finally, my voice still hoarse.

"But I didn't tell you where the crash site is."

I sigh. I've been working with NTSB investigators for almost a year now, yet Mark hasn't gotten used to what I see.

"I know where it is," I say calmly. "An old growth forest northwest of me." I can smell the tang of pine nettles and the raw stench of fire. And I see the blackened furrows and broken trees, the long, white plane a greenstick fracture poking through the earth's brown skin.

"We can't find the box and the little girl's critical. The tower thinks it was pilot error. What went wrong?"

I clutch the receiver. "We'll know soon enough," I say and hang up the phone.

———

THE MORNING COOLNESS mists the fir trees and frames the highway. It swirls ominously across the twisty road that winds through the ancient forest toward the crash site. The heater huffs low, softening the drone of the radio that fills the silence with distraction.

Finally, I reach a roadblock where police cars huddle in the road. The grim-faced officers move almost mechanically in their rain ponchos. A policeman steps toward my car and I roll down the window. He is bleary-eyed from a sleepless night.

"I'm Stacia Evans," I tell him and offer my driver's license. "Investigator Vincent sent for me."

"Yeah, he's expecting you," says the policeman and hands back my license. His gaze falls to the gloves on my hands. "Pull your car off the road over there." He motions toward a small clearing. "You'll have to walk up to the site."

After parking my car, I start up the hillside, bracing myself as I crest the hill and stop.

Torn suitcases and mangled seat cushions, foam and springs erupting, litter the forest floor. Airplane panels lie shattered like egg shells, stark against the nettles and moss blanketing the autumn ground. Bits of fabric and seat belts cling to fir tree branches. Empty plane seats twist around tree trunks and crumple against blackened ground. I suck in a breath, but it hangs in my throat at the rows of yellow body bags lining the horizon. Slowly, I move deeper into the crash debris. At my feet is a torn, sooty tennis shoe. Just one.

Stale smoke scent is cold in the gray drizzle that has started early today. A crane squeaks nearby, loading hunks of gutted plane onto a flatbed truck. One chugs past me and lurches down the hill. I fight the urge to reach down and pick up the lone shoe. Not yet. Not until I've seen everything.

Yellow hazard suits weave through the old forest, investigators combing wreckage for clues – and the black box. A sandy-haired man, looking all of his thirty-five years, moves through the damp forest toward me.

"Stacia," he calls. "Glad you're here."

Mark Vincent's angular chin is stubbled and smudged with dirt, his blue eyes dull. His rain-dappled hazard suit creaks as he extends his hand. I hesitate then shake his hand quickly, trying to avoid images that will haunt me for weeks. They always do.

I nod toward the investigators and cleanup crews. "Have they recovered the bodies?"

"What's left of all two hundred." He glances at the crane raising one of the engines onto another flatbed. "When will you want to start?"

The hazy image of an old woman slips up from a section

of crushed seats. Her steely hair is swept back in harsh curls that reveal deep wrinkles furrowing her brow and cheeks. Her blue pantsuit is spattered with blood and dirt as she flits between workers. She reaches out to them, her misty face a mask of confusion, but they just walk past. Behind her, a young man in a torn rugby shirt and jeans crouches. He stares blankly at ruptured plane panels and luggage strewn everywhere.

A child rushes toward her mother and falls into a ghostly embrace.

The pilot walks grimly behind the investigators and surveys the damage. He grips the arm of his younger copilot, shaking his head and rubbing his eyes.

One by one, the passengers find each other and many go on, disappearing into the woods until I stand alone in the debris.

I watch them all as they search. They cling together while the last broken remnants of their lives are swept away, leaving them only this drizzly hillside – and each other.

Even ghosts collect their dead.

"Stacia?"

A hand waves in front of my eyes and I glance up. Mark steps closer, concern on his face.

"You look like you're about to pass out." He steers me toward a pickup truck where I climb onto the open tailgate and let my muddy boots dangle. Mark slides a warm cup of coffee into my gloved hands.

He stares out at the debris. "You never get used to seeing things like this."

I shake my head and watch two hundred ghosts slipping in and out of the wreckage and I nod.

Now, a woman in a denim dress stands at the center of the wreckage, her gaze encompassing the forest and debris. In her eyes, I see panic. She calls out, but the sounds are lost in the whir of the crane, the buzz of trucks. Finally, her gaze falls to me. The graying, stuffed bear dangling from her hand makes me realize why she waits. I sigh.

"They're all so lost," I mumble, mostly to myself.

"Yeah," says Mark, "two hundred of them lost."

"I meant after the crash. It's not quite over for them yet. Not until they're finished here. It's important to them."

He stares uncertainly at me. I know he tries to see what I see. He never knows what to make of it, but he believes me. He stares at the broken plane and I know he sees nothing beyond the hazard suits and the drizzle.

"What do you mean – important?" he asks.

Sometimes, it really doesn't make any sense. Why some people survive and others die. I remember a cold autumn morning so painfully close to this one. The spray of hot jet fuel burning my flesh, the choking billows of black smoke smothering the dark compartment. I gasp, shoving that bit of broken memory away from me. It's a place I haven't gone in a long while, but the specter remains, cold and dark inside me. Like this gift of mine.

"How's the little girl?" I ask, changing the subject.

"Weaker. Still hasn't regained consciousness."

I rise from the truck and set down my cup. Then I move into the heart of the crash.

I WANDER with the ghosts through the rubble until the investigators and crew thin out. There is a closeness about these souls. They gather together, helping each other. At times, I feel like an intruder, but they accept my presence because I accept theirs.

I move toward the body bags and piles of luggage that have been moved back. Bending down, I pick up a black purse and that lone shoe. I run my hands across the purse and my eyes well with tears. Twenty-two C and D. An elderly couple. Toward the wing, they'd insisted the travel agent seat them there. It's safest over the wing. Inside the purse are the boarding passes. I run my finger over them, catching wisps of excitement and exhaustion – twinges of apprehension at so much money spent to fly. The shoe belongs to a 50-year-old account executive in 2A who just had a surprise birthday party and was returning home.

When I glance up, the elderly couple stands before me, bewildered and shaking their heads. The account executive stands beside them, his other tennis shoe clean and white. I reach out to them. I can't touch them, but they understand my gesture.

"Tell me, please," I say. "What happened?"

"It was so fast," says the elderly man, his voice thin and tight. His ruddy, hooked nose flattens as he talks. "One of the engines on the right side caught fire. The other one just stopped."

"The flight attendants told us to put our heads down and we just prayed," says the woman. "Now, we're here. Why?"

I shake my head. I have no answers for her.

The account executive shoulders past the older man. "The lights went out. Then a flight attendant whispered that one of the engines had stopped working." His gaze falls to the shoe I hold.

The woman's husband takes her hand. She turns toward him. Gently, the elderly man lays a hand against the account executive's sleeve and the younger man nods. Together, they walk out of the wreckage and disappear into the forest.

I see the pilot and move toward him. The investigators watch me as if I'm insane. Ignoring them, I drop down beside the pilot.

"Captain? Can you tell me what happened?"

"Engine failure." His voice is gravely and low, the pain thick in his words. "One of them ignited. The extinguishing systems didn't kick in either. Then we suffered a massive power loss and everything went off-line." He points somewhere in the distance. "I tried to land her in the clearing over that ridge, but we dropped too fast." He shakes his head, his ghost fingers gripping his brown hair. "Some of us might have made it. What have I done?"

I lay my hand against the air where his shoulder would have been. "Your best. Captain, you had no engines. You were over mountains and forest. You did your best. But the tower suspects pilot error. That's why I'm here. You've got to help me find the black box, Captain."

His lined face lifts toward me. "They can't find it?"

I shake my head.

"And they think it's my fault?"

"Not if we can find the black box. Can you help?"

"I'll call my crew together," he says urgently, rising from the ground. Having a purpose stirs him to action. "We'll find it." He flits toward his crewmembers, but stops and turns to me again. "How long do we have?"

I smile. "As long as it takes."

Soon, I'm alone in the debris again. I pace the rows of body bags that are being loaded into trucks. Shortly, the bodies will be carried away to next-of-kin. I reach down and touch a few of the bags, 14B, 6A, 26A – Seattle, Buffalo,

Phoenix. So many stories, so many places . . . so many ripples. They play behind my eyes, a granddaughter going to her grandparents' fiftieth anniversary, a couple on vacation, a woman going to a wedding. I see their stories as if they are my own and it chokes me up. I inhale sharply and continue to pace.

I glance toward the trees and realize I'm not alone. The woman in denim still waits. Ten years fold back like the ragged plane panels at my feet and the image of another plane crash makes me shiver. I was ten. As someone shoved me out of the burning wreckage, I looked back, expecting it to be my mother stumbling out behind me. But it wasn't. I never saw my mother again. Even now, I can't help but wonder if she stood in that wreckage like this woman, searching for me, calling to me.

———————

IT's nightfall when the captain and his crew emerge from the woods. He surges toward me, his frame pearly white against the darkening forest.

"We found it! It's here!"

"Take me there."

He nods.

"Mark, I know where to find the box."

I'm surprised by the calmness of my voice. In moments, Mark Vincent, flanked by a handful of investigators, rushes toward me. I nod at the captain and he hurries into the woods. I follow, the others not far behind.

The captain leads me across the nettle-laden ground,

deeper and deeper. His ghostly gleam is my only guidance. There, battered and hidden by brush, lies the small orange casing of the black box. I tear at the brush, pulling away branches and leaves until I have uncovered the box.

I step back as the investigators descend on it, gently lifting it from the foliage and carrying it back to the site. Mark hovers beside me. I walk behind the investigators as they carry the box out toward the trucks.

When I reach the site, I see the woman in denim still waiting. I close my eyes for a moment, feeling a closeness that makes my chest ache, and approach her. The woman holds the stuffed bear against her chest.

"Have you seen my daughter, Brittany?" asks the woman. "I've been looking for her for hours!" Her ghostly face is tear-streaked and she looks utterly lost. "Please, where is my daughter?"

"She's in a hospital," I answer, my voice thin. "She survived the crash."

"Oh, thank God," the woman cries and slumps to the ground, clutching the bear. Her relief is overwhelming. "Thank God she's safe."

Shards of memories stab back into focus. A voice long-dead calls my name through the roar of fire, through shrill screams. But never have I been so far from that voice as I was that chilly October morning. Ten years have passed, but I clench my eyes closed, my mother's voice haunting my memory. How she shouted at me from the plane's burning wreckage, but they couldn't get to her in time. I inherited my curse that morning. Now, I relive every jet crash as if it were that awful October morning outside Spokane.

I drop to my knees, a sob tearing at my throat. I never saw my mother again. Never got to tell her goodbye. Why didn't she hear me? I called and called, but she never answered. If only she could have followed my voice to the exit. If only ice hadn't formed on the wings. My sobs wrench free, the rain pounding the ground now. If only.

WHILE MARK and the others carry the black box toward a truck, Brittany walks out of the woods. Her form is translucent, milky and soft like fairy dust. I am afraid to move. I crouch there in the pouring rain.

"Mommy?"

The woman turns, her face contorting. "Oh, no! Oh, no, Brittany. I thought you were safe."

Her mother runs toward her and clasps the child to her chest. Sobbing, the little girl holds onto her mother. "I couldn't find you, Mommy. I couldn't find you!"

"Sssh, honey. It's all right." She lays the bear in Brittany's arms.

Shortly, Mark's cell phone rings. I watch the heaviness in his face. He shakes his head. A battle lost. He rushes into the debris and drops down beside me.

"The little girl passed away a few minutes ago," he shouts above the rain.

I nod and watch the last of the ghosts of flight 1155 melt into the woods and fade into the air. For a moment, Brittany's mother remains. She gazes at me as if she knows about my mother. There are no answers to these whys – to my whys – just acceptance, I realize.

"Could you –" I stop in mid-sentence.

She moves toward me and nods, urging me to continue.

"Could you tell my mother – that I miss her?"

"I'm sure she's already heard you."

The woman takes hold of her daughter's hand and slips after the others.

Peace settles warm and calm against my shoulders, as if someone has put an arm around me. My hands stop hurting. I pull off my gloves. The burns are receding . . . my gift is fading. I feel it. And for the first time, I understand this gift.

I've been hearing my mother's voice for ten years – through these images. They were the goodbyes she never got to tell me.

I step out of the wreckage, knowing that tonight, I leave my gift behind. I trudge toward the investigators as they load the black box bound for D.C.

"They'll find that all engines failed," I tell them. "One engine caught fire and the other stopped working. The fire extinguishing system failed to come on-line, too. There was no evidence of pilot error. Goodnight."

I don't even turn to see their expressions. It doesn't matter if they believe me or not. They have the plane's flight record and I have mine. As I climb into my car, I look back at the forest and I wonder if a sparrow falls, does it rise again and sing?

ANNIE REED

Professional writer Annie Reed writes stories that span genres and are always powerful. In fact with Annie, you just never know the type of story you might be reading, but you will always know it will grab you and be a compelling read.

This murder mystery is a great example.

So far Annie has had a story in every issue of this magazine and as the editor, I hope to continue that streak.

Annie's stories have appeared in four best mystery stories of the year volumes so far. Look for so much more of Annie's work at her website https://anniereed.wordpress.com/

THE BLOOD-RED LEAVES OF AUTUMN

ANNIE REED

Two kids found the body lashed to a silver maple. They'd snuck into the tree farm on a dare, two preteen boys playing grab-ass among the blackberry brambles and creeping vines that grew at the base of the trees while the starfield rotated endlessly overhead.

Station B-31861 didn't have a coroner or a detective or even an official cop, just one doctor and a skeleton crew of security officers. The security officers spent their time dealing with petty theft and malicious mischief and breaking up the occasional fistfight. Even highly educated botanists and engineers got bored after enough time stuck in space tending the station's living archives devoted to plants of the North American continent. They played practical jokes on each other, got drunk on the twenty-second century version of the same moonshine their ancestors had brewed, and screwed each other. Eventually some of them had kids who were even more bored than their parents.

Kids hadn't been part of the original plan for Station B-31861, but human beings rarely stuck to the plan. If they had, Station B-31861 and all its sister stations wouldn't still be orbiting Earth, waiting decade after long decade for the world's politicians and mega-corporations and religious zealots to agree on exactly how to reverse centuries of abuse to the planet's fragile ecology so that the plants and animals in the living archives and the people who tended them could return home.

If the ecological disasters could even be reversed. Wallace Beckett was head of security. He didn't know the science. He just had faith that someday it would all work out.

He crouched next to what was left of the body, trying to ignore the stench coming off the remains. The dead woman had been there a while. Her wrists had been tied together and yanked up over her head, then fastened to the silver maple's trunk. The thin synthetic twine used to bind her wrists and her torso to the tree had sunk into the wood as the tree grew, the bark overlapping the twine in places.

Even a layman knew it took a while for a tree to do something like that.

"Know who she is? Or was?"

The question came from the station's director, Lyzette Golden. She was the only true administrator on the station, and the only other person in the farm with Beckett. The division heads were part-time administrators. Their primary functions remained scientific. Station directors like Golden oversaw supply runs, scheduled crew rotations, and arranged VIP tours, all with the assistance of a lone human clerk. An AI could probably do the job just as well, but Golden put a human face on B-31861 at all the official functions sponsored by the global consortium that owned B-31861 and all her sister stations.

Beckett didn't technically report to Golden. The consortium oversaw all security personnel on the stations. In theory that kept Beckett and his crew independent from any directives Golden might want to impose that would hinder his job, but the consortium was headquartered on Earth. Golden might not have any direct authority over him, but Beckett had always tried to treat her with the kind of respect her title deserved.

"I was about to ask you the same question," he said. He'd pinged the division head in charge of the tree farm to see if the man knew who the dead woman was, but so far he hadn't responded.

The tree farm, like all the farms on Station B-31861, was a pest-free environment. That meant no maggots, no beetles, no creepy crawlies to feast on the dead woman's flesh. What was left of her was a decomposed mess. The stench overwhelmed the rich loamy scent of healthy growing things. If the body had been left in one of the farms where food for the station was grown—farms that actually required a human presence on a regular basis—the smell alone would have alerted crew to the body long ago. The tree farm required far less human attention.

Those two kids would be having nightmares for weeks. He knew he would.

Golden leaned closer to the body. She'd put on a thin environmental suit, probably to keep out the smell. Wallace hadn't. He'd smeared ointment beneath his nose that kept out most odors he encountered in his job, like vomit, but the oint-ment wasn't designed to handle something like this.

"No identifying marks on her clothes that I can see," Golden said. "I sent for the doctor to see if we can get a DNA match."

Not to mention cause of death. The remains of her head didn't look bashed in, and there were no obvious burn marks that could have been made by tools the engineers used for station maintenance on what was left of the rest of her. That was the limit of what Beckett could tell just from looking at the body.

He was out of his depth, and he knew it. Golden probably did too. Security officers weren't trained to investigate murders, and that's clearly what had happened here. The dead woman hadn't tied herself to the tree.

"Anyone miss a shuttle in the last few weeks?" he asked.

Station B-31861 had a crew complement of over a thou-sand, most of whom tended the more labor-intensive of the hundred farms contained in the rotating rings arrayed around the station's central core. No one had reported any missing crewmembers. Reports like that were routed to security.

It was possible that a crewmember who was rotating off the station could have missed their shuttle back to Earth. Golden tracked the comings and goings as new crew came on board to replace crewmembers who'd decided not to renew their yearly contracts, although her clerk probably handled most of it. If Golden routinely sluffed off too many of her responsibilities onto her clerk, slipups could happen. Over-worked people made mistakes.

"No one missed a shuttle," Golden said. "I checked on the

way here. If she's one of the crew, someone's been logging reports and doing assignments she should have been covering. No pings from the system."

Reviewing crew logs wasn't part of Golden's job. The system only notified her if scheduled logs weren't updated. If the division heads didn't take care of the problem themselves, it fell to Golden to remind the errant crewmember that failure to perform their assigned tasks had far greater consequences for the future of the planet than simply forgetting to watch grass grow.

"You said 'if' she's crew," Beckett said. "What else could she be?"

He couldn't remember the last time the station had any visiting VIPs. The farms on the B stations just weren't a big enough draw for celebrities and billionaires who could not only afford to pay their way into space for themselves and their entourage but also pay a hefty fee to the consortium for the privilege of getting a personal tour.

The A stations were the ones that got all the attention. Billionaires didn't have a problem spending the kind of money necessary to tour a station where they could see elephants and rhinos and buffalo and a million other species preserved in the habitats on the A stations.

Golden straightened up and stretched her back. "Some people have been here a very, very long time," she said without looking him in the eye. "They've learned how to keep their dirty little unauthorized secrets."

"Unauthorized" was admin-speak for anything not in the original plans for operation of the stations. Brewing alcohol on farmland was unauthorized. Gambling was unauthorized.

Bribing shuttle pilots to hide contraband substances in supply runs was unauthorized.

Children were unauthorized.

Beckett couldn't suppress his astonishment. What she was implying seemed more impossible than a crewmember who'd failed to show up for a scheduled shuttle ride back to Earth.

"You think she's... what, someone's hidden child?" he said.

Was such a thing possible? Children might be unauthorized, but they were still registered in the system.

The leaves on the creeping vines that ran along the ground had begun to turn red. Long ago the botanists in charge of designing the farms had determined the plants they housed would have a better chance of surviving in space if their environment mimicked Earth's seasons as much as possible. The air in the farm felt crisp, the climate-controlled humidity sharp against Beckett's skin, but that wasn't what sent chills down his spine.

Autumn in space. It shouldn't be possible, but it was. Beckett lived every day with things that would have seemed impossible two hundred or even one hundred years ago. B-31861 had been in existence for generations. The trees in this farm were mature, the blackberry brambles thick and overgrown.

Beckett couldn't rule out the possibility that the dead woman was someone's unregistered child. Food wasn't rationed. The station grew more than enough food to support the crew, and the water processing system supported the farms and the crew with ease. Crew movements weren't tracked beyond an ancient keycard system that allowed authorized crewmembers access to the restricted areas in the station, which was pretty much everywhere except recreational facilities and dining areas. Hacking the keycards apparently wasn't all that difficult. The two preteens had managed it.

"We won't know who she was until the doctor gives us a report," Golden said, "but don't discount the possibility." She gave him a hard stare through the thin skin of her environmental suit. "One thing I do know is someone killed this poor woman. That someone might still be on this station, or they might have rotated out by now. I don't want a killer on my station, Wallace. Am I making myself clear?"

"Yes, sir," he said.

She didn't have to tell him that—technically she didn't have the authority to tell him that—but the fact that she had made him realize she must be making a record. Environmental suits had video and audio recording capabilities, and the tree farm didn't have audio or video surveillance equipment. Beckett had been making his own photographic record of the scene, but hers would be far more complete.

She hadn't put the suit on just to avoid the stench. She was covering her ass. If that was the case, she'd taken a big risk giving him as much information as she had.

Just what was going on here? And what, exactly, did she know that she wasn't telling him?

———

"CAUSE OF DEATH WAS A BROKEN NECK."

Emilia Sopa sat in a chair next to the blessedly empty

exam table. Whatever she'd done with the body, at least Beckett didn't have to look at it.

Dr. Sopa was currently the only doctor on the station. The station's other physician had rotated out only six months into a twelve-month contract. He'd forfeited the hefty bonus he would have been paid at the end of a normal rotation just to get the hell off the station. Not everyone was cut out for life in space.

Emilia Sopa had been on the station nearly thirty years, far longer than Beckett's eight. Unlike her departed colleague, she was apparently content with a life that consisted of treating minor injuries, performing the occasional routine surgical procedure, and delivering babies. Any crewmember who developed a serious medical condition was immediately released from their contract and shipped back to Earth.

"What else can you tell me?" Beckett asked.

"She was dead before she was tied to that tree." Sopa called up a screen and squinted at the readout. "The long bones in her arms and legs showed signs of past trauma." She glanced at him. "Never treated in this office."

"Trauma? You mean broken?"

"I mean trauma. Evidence of scoring by sharp objects in multiple places."

She closed the screen with an abrupt movement of one hand and leaned back in her chair, her face impassive, but Beckett could see the anger in her dark eyes. She was furious and trying to contain it.

"This woman was systematically abused over a period of time," she said. "Repeatedly stabbed with an object sharp enough to damage her bones without breaking them. Wounds like that should have been attended to by a physician. They weren't. I ran her DNA. She was never treated by any medical personnel on this station."

Beckett's stomach roiled, but Sopa wasn't finished.

"She was put on display after she was dead." Sopa's dark eyes practically blazed with the force of her anger. "Whoever killed her could have buried her. There's certainly enough soil in the farms on this station to bury a body—hell, the undergrowth in that particular farm would have hidden the body even if she wasn't buried—but they tied her to that damn tree instead and left her there. Abusing her for years wasn't enough."

Beckett swallowed hard against the bile he could feel building at the back of his throat. Sopa had removed the body from the tree farm, and she'd not only noticed something he hadn't, she'd reached a conclusion he hadn't thought of. He told himself it was because he hadn't known the woman was dead before she'd been tied to that tree, but it didn't help.

He had to clear his throat before he felt like he could trust his voice. "How long has she been dead?"

This time Sopa didn't consult her notes. He had a feeling she hadn't needed to before, that she'd only called up the screen to give herself time to try to control her emotions.

"I can't give you time of death," she said, "but given the decomposition, I'd say two to three months. I'll have to review the farm's hydration records, temperature variations. Consult with the botanists who work that farm to determine how long it would take for that tree to grow enough bark to cover the bonds. At this point, I'm not sure I want to do that."

Beckett almost asked her why, but then he got it.

The dead woman's body had been left on display in the tree farm for a purpose. The only people who would have seen it—who would have gotten whatever message the killer had meant to send—were the botanists assigned to work there.

Beckett didn't know how often the botanists actually accessed the farm itself, but he was going to find out.

"You said you ran her DNA," he said. "Did you get an I.D.?"

Just because she'd never been treated in the medical office didn't mean her DNA wouldn't be on record with the station.

"No match," Sopa said. "And before you ask, I ran her DNA against current crew and those who rotated out within the last five years. I didn't have to run it against visitors. The station had none during that time period."

"Why five years?"

"This woman was in her early twenties at the time of death," she said. "The station doesn't accept crewmembers under eighteen years of age, and children below eighteen aren't allowed to tour the station, so there was no need to check any earlier tours."

New crewmembers weren't allowed to bring children with them. The only children living on the station were those who'd been born here.

The sick feeling in Beckett's stomach was eating his guts alive. He had to know if Golden was right, if the dead woman had been a crewmember's child.

"Run her DNA against current crew and those who rotated out within the last twenty-five years," he told Sopa.

"Twenty-five years? I told you—" she began, but Beckett cut her off.

"This time you're not going to be looking for her," he said. "You'll be looking for her parents."

———————————

KENNETH McGWIRE, Division Head for the crew of botanists assigned to work the tree farm, blustered into Beckett's office an hour after Beckett left Dr. Sopa to her DNA research on the dead woman's parentage.

Like all the offices on B-31861, Beckett's office had just enough room for a comfortable chair that automatically adjusted to the contours of his body, a desk that held controls for the holo-screens that floated over the desk's surface, and a single visitor chair. Only in Beckett's case, he'd removed the standard visitor chair and replaced it with a reclining lounger.

Space for crew on the station was limited. Most crew quarters housed more than one person. Only a few division heads or people who'd had children got quarters of their own.

Beckett's eight years on the station didn't qualify him for his own quarters.

While he'd liked most of the security crew he'd shared living space with, more and more often these days he needed time to himself. The reclining lounger gave him a private place to sleep.

He'd added a few other touches to the office to make it feel more like a home, like the holo-screens he'd placed on the walls. Currently two of those screens displayed images of Earth as seen from the station. A third displayed a forest scene complete with clear blue sky, mature pines and healthy aspens, and a gurgling brook of clear water.

The holo must have been taken more than a century ago. He'd found the image in the station's computer database under the file name "Hope." Beckett supposed the name came from what the scientists on the living archives hoped to achieve one day—a return to the natural beauty of the Earth of the past.

Beckett preferred to think of the image as "Belief." Hope was ephemeral, something that could easily be dashed. Belief let him think that the years he'd devoted to this station in support of a common goal hadn't been wasted.

McGwire shot a look at the reclining chair, but he didn't sit in it. "What the hell's the idea of locking my crew out of the farm?" he said.

McGwire was one of those wiry little men who thought belligerence made up for a lack of height, and rudeness was an adequate substitute for respect. Attitudes like that didn't work for Beckett. He deliberately ignored McGwire and kept scrolling through the information on his screen.

"I asked you a question," McGwire said.

"And I pinged you earlier." Beckett minimized the screen without shutting it off. "You chose not to reply. Mind telling me why?"

McGwire had started to lean toward Beckett, but now he shifted his weight backwards. "I was in the middle of a process that couldn't be interrupted."

"A process." Beckett kept his expression impassive.

"You didn't answer my question," McGwire said. "What the hell is so important—"

"Let me show you something," Beckett said, cutting McGwire off before the man could really work up a good head of steam.

Beckett touched a control on his desk. The image on the holo-screen to McGwire's right changed from the image of Earth as seen from space to an image of the dead woman tied to the silver maple in McGwire's tree farm.

McGwire's face had started to flush with anger, but when he looked at the dead woman, the color leeched away and his skin turned gray. He made a choking sound deep in his throat.

"I pinged you to ask if you know who this woman is," Beckett said calmly, "and why her body was left in your farm."

McGwire rubbed the back of one hand across his mouth. "That's my...?" He closed his eyes. "You say you found her in my farm?"

"She's been there for some time," Beckett said. "You want to tell me why no one noticed her until today?"

He didn't add that two kids had found her. McGwire didn't need to know that kids had managed to hack keycards to the farm. Beckett planned on handling that little problem himself. It just wasn't a high priority right now.

McGwire gave his head a little shake, like he was trying to reboot his brain. When he looked away from the screen toward Beckett, his eyes were haunted. "I've never seen anything like that before in my life. I need a…" He cleared his throat and started again. "What did you ask me?"

"Why your systems didn't find her. Why none of your crew discovered her before she looked like that." Beckett jabbed a finger at the holo-screen.

McGwire closed his eyes for a long moment. "That's a mature section of the farm," he said, eyes still closed. "It's basically a forest. It doesn't require a lot of attention. Light, heat, moisture, that's it. That's all the systems keep tabs on." He opened his eyes. It looked like he was making an effort to keep his gaze on Beckett and away from the holo-screen. "We cut back the vines once they go dormant, process the material for mulch, but we won't hit that section for a couple more weeks."

If the woman had been placed on display for a reason, the killer must have known the crew's schedule. And that meant the killer hadn't expected her to be found just yet. They'd deliberately put her body in a place where no one would see—or smell—her until McGwire's crew went in to trim the vines.

So why was McGwire complaining about his crew being locked out of the farm?

Instead of asking directly, Beckett decided to take a different approach. "The farm's a crime scene. I'll have to keep it shut down for the next few days, maybe as long as a week. Will that be a problem for your crew?"

McGwire's eyes flickered away from Beckett's face. "We have processes," he said.

"Processes?" Beckett asked. "Like the one you were stuck in when I pinged you earlier?"

"Experiments," McGwire said, biting off the word. Now that his initial shock was over, some of his earlier belligerence was coming back. "We call them processes in my division."

Beckett nodded. "And you need to access the farm for those processes?"

"Part of it."

"Tell me what part, and I'll see what I can do."

McGwire's nostrils flared. He was clearly a man who wasn't used to having his authority questioned, but he called up a portable screen that displayed a map of the farm. A small section close to the access door the preteens had used was outlined in red. It didn't include the silver maple where the dead body had been found, but it was damn close. Close enough for whoever was conducting the experiments to notice her?

"Who's doing the experiments?" Beckett asked.

"I am." McGwire closed the map. "With the assistance of one of my crew."

Had the body been put on display for McGwire? He wasn't the killer. His reaction to the image of the body had been genuine. People couldn't fake shock like that.

"I need to finish my own process of the scene," Beckett said, "then you can have access."

"How long will that take? These things can't wait."

Beckett leaned back, the contours of his chair reshaping themselves to the change in his position. He planned to walk not only the scene, but the entire section of the farm where McGwire wanted access.

"I'll need the name of the crewmember who'll be assisting you, along with the names of the crew you've assigned to cut back the vines in that section," Beckett said.

McGwire's eyes narrowed. "You don't think one of my crew..."

"I'm investigating a crime," Beckett said, "involving a farm your crew has access to. At this point, I believe the term is 'person of interest.' The sooner you get me those names, the sooner you can have access."

McGwire glared at him, but he left without saying another word.

Only after he was gone did Beckett realize McGwire hadn't answered the most important question of all.

Did he know who the dead woman was?

And if he did, did that mean he knew who'd killed her?

IT TOOK McGwire nearly an hour to send the names of his crew to Beckett. The delay made Beckett wonder if McGwire had made any last-minute adjustments to his crew assignments.

Beckett had already looked up all of McGwire's six-person crew. No married couples, no registered partners, and no registered children among them. McGwire had been on the station nineteen years, scrabbling his way up the promotion ladder until he'd been appointed division head twelve years ago after the previous division head rotated out. The remainder of his crew had been on the station anywhere from two to twelve years, with nothing remarkable in their records.

Most of the botanists who spent the kind of time on the station that McGwire had switched farms over the years as a way of combating boredom. Not McGwire. He'd stayed with the tree farm for his entire career. He probably thought of the farm as his own private woodland preserve. No wonder he'd been so pissed off when Beckett locked him out.

Beckett had been walking the scene in the tree farm when he'd received the information from McGwire. He'd entered by the same access door the preteen boys had used, but he still had to hike a good ten minutes to get to the silver maple.

When he'd first been assigned to the station, he'd tried to memorize all the pertinent facts about each of the farms, but there was just too much information. Each of the farms was over twenty-five square kilometers, complete with hillocks and dips and trails and thousands of varieties of plants.

The rotation of the rings provided the farms with as close to Earth normal gravity as possible. Overhead lighting was programmed to deliver the optimum sunlight equivalent, and hydration systems provided a combination of ground water and mist in the air, all calculated to nurture whatever plants grew in each farm.

Dr. Sopa might have been right about there being more than enough dirt on the station to bury a body, but the task would have been difficult, if not downright impossible, in this section of the tree farm. The vines caught his feet and the blackberry brambles scratched his hands and arms as he made his way to the silver maple. The ground was covered with fallen leaves, and when he tried to dig at the dirt with the toe of one boot, he dug through more leaves than dirt.

The first time he'd been here, he'd been too intent on the body—on the pure shock of it—to fully take in the scene itself. This particular silver maple was set apart from the others in the little grove. It looked like an afterthought, shorter than the other trees, like something that wasn't planned but merely happened, and the botanists had left it alone.

Was that part of the message? A death that wasn't planned? Or had it been the life that wasn't planned?

Sopa said the woman was dead when she was bound to the tree. Had she been killed here? He'd taken images of the crime scene, but he hadn't been looking for signs of a struggle. And even if there'd been a struggle, would signs of it still be here after two or three months? The vines and brambles were living, growing things.

He toed the ground again, disturbing some of the red leaves that had fallen from the vines. He was frustrated with himself, with his lack of training for a situation like this. The woman, whoever she'd been, deserved better than she was getting from him.

A ping sounded in his right ear. He was getting a call from Dr. Sopa.

"What do you have for me?" he asked.

Her image didn't appear as a little hologram floating in front of him. The call was voice only, unusual for official communications.

"Come see me," she said. "But not in my office." She gave him the location of one of the dining rooms in an inner hub of the station. "Twenty minutes," she said. "I won't wait for you if you're late." Then she signed off.

It had taken Beckett ten minutes to hike into the farm. He'd just barely make it if he left right away.

Leaves had stuck to the toe of his boot. He didn't want to track leaves all over the station. He bent over to brush the leaves off, and that's when he saw a glint of white beneath the red leaves on the ground.

He slipped a clear glove over his hand before he dug through the leaves to retrieve the object, taking images as he went. He already knew what he'd found, but he held the object up anyway, making sure he took images of all sides.

It was a broken key card, cracked down the middle and caked with bits of leaves and dirt.

And the chip that made it work, that would have identified the owner of the card, was missing.

THE DESIGNERS of the stations realized that crew stuck in space for extended periods of time would need places to blow off steam. Not simply exercise rooms with equipment that worked well in the less than Earth normal gravity of the inner rings where the crewmembers lived, but places where the crew could gather and eat together, drink together, or watch entertainment vids together.

The public dining room Dr. Sopa had chosen for a meeting place was in one of the station's smaller recreational areas. The menu was limited to sandwiches and salads, the drinks to a variety of coffees and teas, and the tables were industrial-grade white plastic bolted to the floor. The chairs were not quite as comfortable as Beckett's office chair, but they could be adjusted to allow crewmembers to sit at varying heights and distances from the table.

Sopa was already sitting at a two-person table near the rear of the dining room when he got there. She had a mug of something hot and steamy on the table in front of her, and her hands were wrapped around the lidded container.

"Do I have time to grab something?" Beckett asked. He hadn't had a meal since breakfast, and it was nearing the end of his normal day. Not that anything had been normal on this day.

She looked up at him, and he was startled by the haunted look in her dark eyes. "You won't want anything. I'm not sure I'm ever going to eat here again."

Beckett had intended to at least get a mug of his favorite tea, an oolong blend usually only in stock for a short period of time after the station received a shipment of supplies from Earth. The last shuttle had been two weeks ago, and the tea was due to run out any day now. Instead, he sat down in the chair across from Sopa.

"What the hell did you find out?" he asked.

She glanced over her shoulder as if to double-check that no one was within earshot. The dining room was nearly deserted, with only the crewmember who processed the food orders standing behind a half-wall at the front of the dining room and two other crew, both botanists from one of the food-growing farms, sitting at a table near the front. A soft instrumental piece was playing over speakers embedded in the steel-gray walls.

The music, together with the fact that the dining room, like the crew quarters, had no video or audio recording devices, gave the crew a sense of privacy, something that was missing from nearly every other part of the station. Especially for the crew who shared their quarters with another crewmember.

Apparently satisfied that no one could overhear them, Sopa turned back to Beckett. "You asked me to run our victim's DNA again for a very specific reason," she said. "I'm not going to say what that is, nor am I going to tell you that I deleted our prior conversation from the station's records."

She was speaking so quietly Beckett could hardly hear her, but he heard enough. His eyebrows shot up and he leaned back in his chair. He felt like she'd slapped him.

Deleting station records wasn't officially possible. He should know. Part of the training for his job had included training on the station's computerized data storage systems, which were extensive, ridiculously redundant, and—according to the designers of the systems—hack proof.

The living archive project was too important to the future of the planet to risk a loss of data. Keeping the farms thriving in space was only part of the project. Most of the work done by the botanists had to do with developing hardier versions of the plants in the farms so that they could thrive on a planet that had become hostile to them.

Apparently Sopa had been on the station long enough to figure out how to delete recordings made in her office. Like their conversation about the dead woman and his request that Sopa look for the woman's parents. There would be no record of their conversation in the dining room, only the fact that they'd both been there at the same time.

If Sopa had figured out how to alter the station's official records, other people on the station could too. Beckett worked among some of the most brilliant minds the consortium could find and convince to spend what might be a significant part of their lives isolated in space.

What else had been deleted from the station's records? Was there even a way to find out? The possibilities made Beckett's blood run cold. If Sopa could alter the records in medical, could the botanists alter the records of their experiments? That didn't make sense, but another reason to alter records did.

In all his years on the station, the only crimes reported to security were petty crimes or heated arguments that had escalated into fistfights. What if those weren't the only crimes committed on the station? What if records of other, more serious crimes, had simply been deleted from the system?

What if someone else had been murdered and all evidence of that murder had simply been erased, the victim reduced to compost or buried deep within the dirt in one of the other farms? Like one of the farms where food was grown for the station?

All of a sudden, he understood Sopa's comment about whether he'd ever want to eat again.

"I will tell you that once you know how to delete a thing," she said, "you also know how to spot when a thing has been deleted." She glanced down at her mug. "I won't tell you that I've learned how to be more careful than most."

She was holding onto her mug so tightly that her knuckles had turned white. The rich aroma of coffee rose with the steam from the opening in the mug's lid. He wondered if her hands were as cold as they looked.

"Data isn't stored in just one place," she said. "When something's deleted, all references to it have to be deleted or the data's still there. If you know where to look."

Beckett thought about all those ridiculously redundant data-keeping systems he'd learned about and mostly ignored, trusting the process to work as it had been designed. His job was security, but in all his years on the station, he'd been focused on the physical safety of the crew. He'd only been doing half his job.

"What the hell did you find?" he asked her again, thinking of Golden's comment about crew who'd been here so long that they knew how to keep their dirty little unauthorized secrets.

Sopa swallowed hard enough that he saw her throat move. "A pattern," she said. "A decades-long pattern. Something that's been going on right under our noses, sight unseen, until someone lashed it to a tree and we discovered it first."

She looked up at him. Her eyes were still haunted, but he saw a hint of the anger she'd had back in her office.

"Take a look at the shuttle manifests," she said. "Cargo weight. Fuel consumption. Station-to-station supply runs."

"What am I looking for?" he asked. If he could even find what she'd found. His training on the station's data-keeping systems had been nearly a decade ago.

Instead of answering him, she got up from the table, and he thought their meeting was over. Then she looked down at him, and he thought she looked older than she had just a few hours ago. Older and incredibly tired.

"All these brilliant minds," she said. "I believed in what they're doing, what we're all doing up here. That's why I stayed, but I've had enough. I thought my colleague was an idiot for taking an early out, and now I'm going to do the same thing. I'm taking the next shuttle and getting the hell out of here."

She left the dining room without another word.

Beckett stared after her for a long moment, then he walked up to the crewmember in charge of the food. He wasn't hungry, but he was going to be working late trying to find whatever had frightened Sopa so badly that she wouldn't tell him even in this place where no one could overhear their conversation. Frightened her so badly that she was fleeing the only home she'd known for nearly thirty years. He doubted he would ever see her again.

At least she'd told him enough to give him a place to start.

If he could make the systems work the way she had. He had to, or somebody who'd worked on this station was going to get away with murder.

AFTER TWO HOURS spent in his office peering at manifests and fuel consumption logs for station-to-station supply runs, Beckett had managed to give himself a tension headache, but he was no closer to discovering what had frightened Sopa.

The broken key card he'd found in the tree farm was a dead end. The card belonged to one of the parents of the preteens who'd broken into the farm. Once the kids had discovered the body and realized what kind of trouble they were in, they'd broken the identity chip out of the card, covered the card with leaves and loose dirt, and thrown the chip as far away from the body as they could.

He'd thought the keycard was an important clue. It wasn't. If he couldn't figure out what Sopa had found, that would mean he'd wasted time running down another dead end. If that happened, there was a strong possibility he'd never find out who'd murdered the dead woman, much less find out who she'd been.

Sopa had specifically mentioned station-to-station supply runs. He'd never had a reason to get involved with those shuttles. The supply runs been instituted long before Beckett had taken the job as head of security for B-31861 as a means to combat a unique—and unexpected—problem.

Thanks to the efforts of the B stations' botanists to improve the hardiness of the plants in the farms, the vegetable farms produced far more than necessary to feed the stations' crew. The A stations had a similar mandate—improve the hardiness of the animals in their living archives. Those efforts were successful enough that the A stations' habitats began to suffer from over-population.

Someone in the consortium got a brilliant idea. Instead of incurring the expense to ship freeze-dried vegetables from Earth to the A stations and preserved meats from Earth to the B stations to fill in the gaps between what the stations produced for themselves and what the crew needed to keep themselves healthy and happy, why not have the stations ship their overflow to each other? Station-to-station shuttles were cheaper to run thanks to lower fuel consumption, which meant the shuttles could run more often.

Problem solved.

Which was why Beckett's turkey sandwich was made with real turkey, and why the crewmembers on the nearby A station had fresh tomatoes and lettuce for their sandwiches.

He put his plate with the remains of his turkey sandwich on his desk and pinched the bridge of his nose. It would help if he knew what leaps of logic Sopa had made. Cargo weight, she'd said. Fuel consumption. On station-to-station shuttles. What did that add up to?

She had to have uncovered something else first. He'd asked her to check DNA for the parents of the murdered woman, and somehow she'd ended up checking station-to-station shuttles.

B-31861's trading partner was A-27430. It was the closest A station, which made for the shortest shuttle run. The manifests and fuel consumption records were available to Beckett as head of security. Golden was in charge of monitoring the shuttle runs, but the logs of those runs had all been approved by her assistant.

Her overworked assistant.

Overworked people made mistakes.

Beckett leaned toward his screens. This time he put up the logs for the last year side by side. On average, the shuttles between the stations ran every week. Looking at them this way, he saw something he'd missed before.

Every so often, the data for fuel consumption and cargo weight was identical from one shuttle originating on A-27430 to another shuttle originating on A-27430, right down to the decimal point.

That couldn't be a coincidence. He hadn't noticed the duplicate data until he'd pulled up the records side by side. He doubted Golden's assistant would have noticed at all before she simply marked them as approved.

Shuttle data was automatically entered into the station's database by the systems on the shuttle. That data was disseminated to a wide variety of places—fuel storage, food storage, meal preparation, and even the systems that tracked the proper mix of gases in the station's air. If someone had erased the actual data by substituting a copy of old data in its place, had they tracked and erased the data from all those various places?

Sopa had talked about deleted records. Had she found the actual records for the shuttles originating on A-27430? And then followed that data until she found something that truly terrified her?

Beckett spent the next three hours diving through the overly redundant data storage systems on the station until he found a small part of what Sopa must have found.

"Son of a bitch," he muttered to himself.

The cargo weight of a station-to-station shuttle originating on A-27430 three months ago had been 52 kilos heavier than the altered log reported.

Fifty-two kilos. The weight of someone like the young woman who'd been killed and left tied to a silver maple in McGwire's farm for him to discover.

———

McGWIRE's STATUS as a division head and his seniority on the station afforded him private quarters. It was the middle of the station's night when Beckett knocked on McGwire's door, but the man opened his door only a few seconds later. He was still dressed in the same clothes he'd been wearing when he blustered into Beckett's office, only now his belligerence was gone.

"I was wondering how long it would take you to put it together," McGwire said. "You surprised me. I thought I had at least another day or two."

He backed away from the door, and Beckett stepped inside.

McGwire's quarters weren't large. Most of the station was devoted to the farms, the labs, and the machinery that kept the stations going decade after decade. Crew quarters were a place to sleep, to shower, maybe have a private communication with any friends or family left behind on Earth or on the other stations.

Communications weren't monitored—private was private —but the station's systems did keep track of the fact that communications had taken place. After Beckett had discovered the weight discrepancy in the shuttle, he'd checked both McGwire's communications data and data concerning the process McGwire had scheduled himself to perform in the farm.

The crewmember McGwire'd said would be assisting him with the process had been added to the schedule after McGwire had left Beckett's office. That must have been part of the reason for McGwire's delay in relaying that information to Beckett.

The other reason for the delay was a communication McGwire'd had with one of the station-to-station shuttle pilots who lived on A-27430.

An open suitcase, half filled with clothes and other personal items, sat on McGwire's bunk. He was leaving too, just like Sopa.

"The dead woman was left as a message for you," Beckett said.

McGwire didn't argue the point. Instead he dropped down

on the bed next to his suitcase like his legs had given out on him. "I didn't kill her."

Beckett already knew that. She'd been killed on A-27430 and shipped to B-31861 like so much dead meat. The logs listed live weight (the pilots) and dead weight (the cargo) as different entries. But she'd been a human being.

"If you didn't kill her, why was she—"

"Because I wouldn't cooperate!"

McGwire's bluster returned so suddenly that Beckett took an involuntary step backward. Beckett had clipped a stunner on his uniform belt before he'd left his office, and his hand dropped instinctively to the stunner's handle.

"The farm's my fucking farm and I wasn't going to pollute it with their failures." McGwire ran his fingers through his hair. "They knew my schedule. Knew I had processes I needed to conduct at the turn of the season. Knew I'd find her and I'd have no choice but to bury her if I didn't want to implicate myself in what they've been doing. 'Get your hands dirty,' he actually said to me."

He slumped forward, fingers laced at the back of his neck. "They're cocky little bastards over there," he said. "Think they're hot shit because they get all the VIP attention. If those VIPs only knew what was really happening in those labs. 'It'll be easier for you the next time,' he said, like I had to just bend over and take it."

The next time. What the hell was actually going on?

"Make me believe you didn't have anything to do with this," Beckett said. "Make me understand."

Without looking up, McGwire started talking. Beckett made sure he captured every word on his own personal recording device, not on the station's system. He didn't want this recording to disappear.

"You know our mandate," McGwire said. "Engineer stronger plants, make them able to thrive on Earth as it is, not as we hope it will be someday. Good old genetic engineering. They have the same mandate on the A stations."

Beckett knew that, but he kept his mouth shut. He didn't want to interrupt McGwire now that the man was talking.

"What most of us don't know is there's a special division on A-27430," McGwire said. "I didn't, not until I made division head. They have the same mandate, only they're trying to improve people. Good old genetic engineering." McGwire's voice hitched. It sounded like a sob.

Beckett's hands felt like ice. McGwire was telling him that A-27430 was not only experimenting with genetic engineering on *people*, but doing it as a mandate from the consortium.

"Clones?" he asked.

"No," McGwire said. "In vitro. They shuttle in volunteers who're assigned somewhere where they're not noticed, young women who need the money, and pay them big bonuses to keep their mouths shut."

McGwire rubbed a hand across his mouth, then he looked at Beckett with eyes as haunted as Sopa's had been.

"You're not a scientist," he said, "so you might not realize the number of failures it takes to get even a partial success. Fail with a plant, you mulch the failure and grow another one. Fail with a person? If you're lucky, it's a miscarriage. If you're not, and the failure doesn't appear until after the baby's born or...after it grows..."

He trailed off, glancing away like he couldn't meet Beckett's gaze. Maybe he couldn't stand the look of disgust, of horror, that Beckett couldn't quite keep off his face.

"They need some way to get rid of the bodies," McGwire said. "The habitat systems on the A stations would record the decomp and send bots to remove the dead animal. Can't have bots finding a dead kid instead of a dead racoon or baby bear. Can't shoot a dead kid out an airlock and have the station's monitoring systems pick it up as space debris. Sure as hell can't recycle the body with animal by-products. The recyclers pick up human DNA, and they can't ship the body back to Earth on a shuttle with crewmembers who have no idea what's going on. So they send their failures here for burial in farms that don't need a lot of attention."

"Like yours," Beckett said.

"Never mine!" McGwire glared at him. "I never allowed that."

Which explained why McGwire had never transferred to another farm. His farm was the only one he knew was clean.

"Tell me about the dead woman," Beckett said.

McGwire shuddered visibly. "She had no pain receptors, that's what he said. They tested her repeatedly."

By stabbing her, among other things. Beckett didn't want to hear what else they'd done to her, but he didn't want McGwire to stop talking.

"At first they thought it was a good thing, but there was something wrong with her brain," McGwire said. "The older she got, the more they couldn't control her. I guess it's hard to run a secret division if the secrets keep trying to escape."

So they'd killed her, or she'd broken her neck trying to get away. Then they'd used her to try to get McGwire to cooperate.

"I'm going to have to report this," Beckett said.

McGwire snorted. "To who? Your bosses? Think it through. These people have a mandate. Where do you think that comes from?"

Beckett felt the blood leave his face. He hadn't thought it through. He was just as screwed as Sopa and McGwire. And probably as screwed as Golden, who'd felt it necessary to make a recording to cover her ass when she told him to make sure the killer wasn't on her station.

McGwire stood up and snapped his suitcase shut. "My suggestion to you," he said, "is to bug out. Just leave. Now that you know what really goes on here, this place will eat your soul if you don't."

Beckett knew this day had already eaten his soul, no matter what he decided to do next.

BECKETT LASTED ANOTHER WEEK.

The day after he'd confronted McGwire, Beckett went to Golden's office to give her an update. He told her that the body had been too degraded to find any useable evidence, and with Sopa gone, he had no hope of getting any additional forensics. It was only a partial lie.

"What about the killer?" she'd asked.

"I found no evidence to indicate this death was anything other than a one-time incident," he said, another lie. "I'm still investigating."

"My assistant will give you all the support you require," she said, a dismissal if he'd ever heard one.

He had no doubt that the official record of their meeting would be deleted, just as he had no doubt she'd made her own private recording of what had been said. He had.

He went through the motions of looking for a missing crewmember who should have caught a shuttle but hadn't, but his heart wasn't in it. He slept poorly, ate poorly, and even turned off the holo-screens on his office wall.

He'd thought briefly about playing the hero. The consortium was the most powerful global entity on Earth, but people needed to know its mandates were killing innocent children. He had no proof of that, but he did have a dead woman.

Or he thought he did.

When he tried to track down what Sopa had done with the dead woman's remains, he discovered that her body was missing. Sopa's autopsy report had been deleted from the station's records.

Whoever had done that got their instructions directly from the consortium, which meant they'd have no qualms dispatching Beckett if he became a problem. They'd bury his body in one of the farms, then alter the station's records to make it look like he'd returned to Earth.

If they killed Beckett, they'd probably kill the two preteens who'd discovered the body. He couldn't do anything for the dead woman, but he could save those two boys.

He still believed the primary work being done on the stations was important to the future of the planet. Was human genetic experimentation moral? His job had always been simply to enforce laws as they existed. That had been his moral compass, but now that compass was broken. A broken man couldn't do the job he was expected to do.

Before he caught the shuttle that would take him back to Earth, Beckett visited the tree farm one last time. The vines were rapidly shedding their leaves now, and the maple's leaves had taken on a blood-red tinge of their own.

Beckett's worst fear was that the consortium had only mandated genetic experimentation on people because they believed Earth wasn't redeemable. Maybe the squabbling among politicians and mega-corporations and religious zealots had gone on too long, and Earth was past the tipping point.

Or maybe the mandate was a *just in case*, worst-case scenario. He had no way of knowing. He didn't know science.

He picked up one of the fallen leaves and tucked it in his pocket. He still had faith in the basic purpose of the stations. The plants and animals in these living archives deserved to be preserved and cared for. Even if Earth would never again be a place where they could thrive.

He patted his pocket then turned to make the ten-minute hike out of the farm.

It all boiled down to hope for the future. He was surprised that his was still intact.

Maybe hope wasn't so ephemeral after all.

KRISTINE KATHRYN RUSCH

Kristine Kathryn Rusch is a New York Times *and* USA Today *bestselling writer and maybe the most award-winning and prolific writer working today. She has won more awards in science fiction and mystery than just about anyone alive and she is the only person to win the Hugo Award for her writing as well as her editing.*

Since this issue has a lot of mystery and crime stories, I figured I would anchor the issue with another by one of the masters of the mystery and crime genre. Enjoy.

You can find out a lot more about Kris's work at her publisher, WMG Publishing Inc www.wmgbooks.com *or her website* www.kriswrites.com

UPDATES

KRISTINE KATHRYN RUSCH

Election night 1984. Steven Blackburn was playing dirges, his prematurely silver head disappearing from the window in Booth One as he bent down to retrieve yet another depressing record. There was no jazz in his show tonight, Marisa thought as she prepped Booth Two. She was moving at hummingbird speed: interview tape on the reel-to-reel, cued up to the first cut; headphones on testing; election night news music in the cart; in the main studio, mikes positioned, paper water glasses in cup holders, phone/interview connection set.

The dirges echoed through the entire radio station. Blackburn was a life-long radical, like most people who worked at the station, but he didn't have to act as if the world had ended just because Ronald Reagan was being re-elected by a landslide.

Marisa whipped off her headphones. She had to return to the newsroom to make sure the last-minute reports were typed and the anchors were ready. Election night for her meant five updates on the hour, from 8 p.m. to midnight. Five newscasts, all new, all important. The station's unique view meant that its election coverage was also unique.

The phone buzzed. She glanced down. Three lights were on, which meant three phone lines active. Blackburn was on one, the receiver pressed between his ear and his shoulder, his headphones askew on his skull; her City Hall feed was on the other, waiting to give the update on the results on the air; and the third was ringing. Ringing, and no one to answer, not with Blackburn talking and cueing up another dirge, and her team racing like greyhounds in the newsroom below.

She punched the button as she picked up the receiver, blurting the station's call numbers in her this-better-be-important tone.

"Someone's going to die tonight," said a nasal male voice.

"What?" she asked, but she was already talking to a dial tone. Great.

All she needed was more stress.

She pressed the intercom. "Steve, you been getting crank calls?"

He hung up the phone, glanced at her, and leaned forward.

"No," he said. "Just people who love the music."

That didn't surprise her. The station was listener-sponsored, and had been founded fourteen years before as a voice of the counterculture. Most of its original listeners still lived in town, and most of them still believed.

"I think I just got a death threat," she said.

"What?"

"Some nut job, saying someone's going to die tonight."

"You call the cops?"

"Should I?"

They stared at each other through two separate windows, the empty studio between them. Blackburn blinked first. One of his dirges was ending.

"It wasn't very specific," he said.

"If it happens again, we'll call the cops."

"Deal." Then he slipped his headphones on, leaned into the mike, and in his silkiest voice, announced the name of the dirge he'd been playing.

Marisa got up, and went through the double soundproofed doors, then into the main hallway. She had argued with the station manager for a receptionist on election night, but had lost. The station ran on volunteer labor. Only the station manager, the program manager, the music director and Marisa, as news director, were paid. Everyone else offered time free of charge.

She ran down the stairs to the newsroom. The basement was dark except for the light pouring out of the newsroom to her left. Broadcast voices mingled: Dan Rather on CBS, some nobody on CNN, Kyle Henderson—a volunteer she trained who now worked for the rival public radio station, and two other locals, all struggling with the latest updates. Beneath it all the dirges blared from speakers mounted against the ceiling.

The room was long and narrow, the floor covered with dirt and slush from the snow shower earlier that day, people crammed into wooden chairs, bodies hunched over stories as they worked on the built-in counter. Five radios, all at least ten years old, were on and scattered about the room. Two black-and-white televisions sat on rickety shelves overhead, and the only color television, with its cable hookup, was tucked into the corner, near her so-called desk.

The UPI machine typed the latest, pausing to beep every few minutes with a warning that whatever it was printing was important.

She ripped off the teletype paper as she went by, depositing it on Kamal's desk so that he could go through for updates. Kamal was a good kid: an incredibly thin college freshman with dreams of becoming a reporter. But he wasn't real versed in local news—having come to the Midwest from the East—and his enthusiasm simply didn't make up for knowledge. She gave him the UPI job because it was the only thing he could do, feel useful, and stay out of her way.

Joseph, her main anchor, finished typing the last of his copy on the black 1920s manual. All the typewriters were donated: she had the only electric, and the station simply couldn't afford to upgrade to computers. Not that anyone would have known what to do with a computer anyway. Most people seemed to be intimidated by them. She knew she was.

"I think I have old stats from the governor's race," Joseph said. His brown eyes were sparkling, his dark hair mussed. He thrived on election night. He was forty, older than the rest of the crew, a medical researcher in real life, but a veteran of the station who'd been volunteering from the beginning. He saw it as a continuation of the work he had begun as one of the original members of the Berkeley Free Speech Movement in '64. She loved working with this team: Joseph; Naomi his co-anchor, an attorney who specialized in Fair Housing; and Rob, a freelance writer who, she suspected, made most of his living selling cocaine. Rob did commentaries that were sharp, penetrating, and to the point. Several other local stations had tried to steal him, but he felt that leaving his volunteer post would be like giving up his soul.

"Compare what you've got with Kamal," Marisa said, "and remember that we'll be getting a live update from City Hall anyway."

City Hall was election central. All the stats poured in there, and the reporters on-site used the pressroom to feed the information back to their stations.

"Kamal," she said. "Make sure you monitor one of the local TV stations for updates, preferably Channel Six. They at least have real newspeople instead of bubbleheads."

A few other volunteers were also in the room, typing furiously on their manuals as well. Election night was always crazy, always busy. The station was located right in the middle of downtown, and she had lined up all the candidates to do drop-ins throughout the night. The first would arrive—she glanced at the oval clock with the sweeping second hand that was perched above the newsroom door—within the half hour.

"Holly," she said to the curly haired volunteer sitting toward the back. "Take your typewriter upstairs and sit at reception. Here's the list of the people we're expecting. Whenever someone shows up, put them in the studio and buzz me."

"Will do, boss," Holly said, picking up the twenty-pound typewriter. As she passed Marisa, Marisa shoved the list into the platen. Then Holly disappeared out the door.

Holly had worked three other election nights, including the disaster in which the governor had waited for fifteen minutes in the entry before someone noticed him. They managed to catch him just before he headed into the night.

Someday, Marisa thought. Someday she'd work at a big fancy station with lots of money and photos of its most famous anchors in a big, glitzy reception area. She would get a real salary, not the measly thing that only allowed her to rent a tiny one-bedroom apartment and required her to budget everything, including meals. But it would also mean losing control to advertisers, allowing her broadcasts to be censored by the brass, and never hearing another dirge again.

"On in two!" Marisa said.

Joseph was up, copy in hand. Kamal handed him a few UPI pages which Marisa snatched so that she could double-check them. She pulled papers out of three different typewriters while the writers were screaming, "No! No! Not yet!" and took Naomi by the arm, helping her out of her chair.

Naomi already had ink on one cheek. Her normally neat hair was tousled, and her lawyer's makeup long gone. Marisa was glad they were radio: her team could never manage the neatness required for television.

"Upstairs, now," Marisa said.

Joseph and Naomi left. Marisa punched line two.

"Still there?" she asked.

"Still here," Douglas, her City Hall reporter, replied.

"Anything good?"

"Not that we didn't expect."

"Keep holding. You'll be on in less than five."

"You said that fifteen minutes ago."

"Are you missing stories by hanging on the line?"

He laughed. It was a joke among the real reporters. Election nights were guaranteed boredom mixed with statistics. "No."

"Then stop bitching." She punched the hold button and hung up the receiver. While she had been talking to him, she had been checking the copy. She threw out one UPI story, hand-wrote the last line for the three stories she pulled out of the typewriters, and arranged the entire update by anchor, putting their names on the top of each page. Then she ran up the stairs, two at a time. She got her exercise here, and for free.

When she reached the top of the stairs, she glanced at the clock. 45 seconds until air, and she hadn't done a sound check. The downfall of volunteer labor was that very few volunteers had the time or talent to learn the fine art of engineering. Even fewer learned how to do complex jobs like a regular newscast. Only three people in the entire station could do something that required finesse, like election nights —and she was one of the three.

"Marisa?" Holly said from the reception desk.

"Make it fast," Marisa said as she took the last few stairs.

"Councilman Adams is in the studio. I set him up and—"

"Is he on mike three?"

"I think so."

"Good." Marisa pushed open the studio door.

"And," Holly said with emphasis. "I got a death threat."

Marisa stopped, glanced at the clock. Thirty seconds. Damn. "It'll have to wait."

"It sounded serious."

"Someone will die tonight?" she asked.

"How'd you know?"

"I got one too. Call the police. Do not use the emergency number. Ask them what they want to do about it."

"Okay."

Marisa pushed through the studio doors, handed the divided copy to Joseph and Naomi, waved at Councilman

Adams, and was at her seat behind the board with ten seconds to spare. She pushed the pot down for a spot check.

"I need levels. Councilman?"

Adams was a pro. He gave her a count with his stentorian voice, and she miked him. She didn't even have to test Joseph and Naomi. She knew their levels instinctively. She double-checked everything, made sure no one touched the reel-to-reel, then watched Steve Blackburn. He grinned at her through the double windows. They both sat higher than the anchors and the councilman.

Blackburn introduced the election update, then pointed at Marisa, who punched the music cart. As the dopey piano lead announced election coverage, Joseph and Naomi turned toward her. Marisa punched on their mikes, eased the music pot down, and cued them at the precise moment when the levels matched.

Joseph and Naomi did their opening routine like the veterans they were, and Marisa lost the next fifteen minutes to opening mikes, cueing phoners, and running tape.

When she finished the segment, and cued Blackburn who started another dirge, her mind was on the next update. She noted Holly's absence from the front desk, but thought little of it. Not until Councilwoman Bader, a former volunteer at the station, poked her head into the newsroom.

"What? Still no greeting committee on election night?"

Marisa had been on the phone with Douglas, debating whether or not to send one of their rookies to the governor's campaign headquarters—and she had been watching the returns on Channel Six—while she was fielding questions from Joseph about the phone interview he was trying to set up with his own personal Deep Throat at the Pentagon.

Marisa put a hand over the receiver. "Sorry. Holly is supposed to be up there. Just head into the studio. You know what to do. And thanks."

The councilwoman grinned and went back up the stairs. She had gotten her start in politics at the station, probably gotten bit with the fever on an election night, and she knew how things went.

"Kamal," Marisa said. "Did Holly have to check out early?"

"She didn't say."

Or no one noticed. Working with volunteers was the bane of her existence.

"Go upstairs and man the desk. We have too many important people filtering in and out tonight to leave it empty."

"But the UPI—"

"I can handle that," Marisa said and thought, *along with every other goddamn thing*. "You just answer the phone, watch the door, and greet everyone who comes in like they're royalty, even if you have no clue who they are."

"Yes, ma'am." He ran up the stairs.

On the bright side, she thought, volunteers were enthusiastic—at least the new ones.

She finished up her phone conversation, glanced through the wire, assigned a few more last-minute stories, told Joseph to forget the Pentagon mole (who seemed convinced that Reagan would bomb Nicaragua that night), argued with him for a few moments, allowed him to get five minutes of tape, in case the bombing actually happened which she knew it wouldn't, and then went upstairs to set up the studio for the next update.

She set up the studio again, checking water for the anchors, replacing the other waters. Councilwoman Bader folded her hands, grinning as she watched.

"Nice to know nothing changes around here."

Marisa grinned back, and pulled the mike closer to Bader's mouth. "You going to be witty?"

"I wasn't up for re-election. I can afford to."

"Good." Then she went back into the booth.

"Marisa?" Blackburn's tinny voice sounded through the intercom. She went to the board, and pressed the intercom button. He was watching her through the double windows. She was glad Bader was looking down. Blackburn looked even worse than he had when the evening started.

"What?"

"I think I just heard from your crank."

"Oh?"

"Yeah. He said something about death and politics."

"I don't have time for this, Steve," Marisa said.

"It was creepy. It was weird."

"Creepy, weird, how?"

"Like a threat."

"I told Holly to call the cops. Did she do it before she left?"

"I didn't see her leave."

The hair rose on the back of Marisa's neck. "What do you mean?"

"She got me a glass of water, and said she'd be back. I thought she was delayed at the desk."

Marisa shook her head. She didn't like how this felt, and she didn't have time to deal with it. "She's been missing for the last half hour. I thought she went home. You know how it is."

Blackburn nodded. He'd been at the station for years. Volunteers often had emergencies at home, or forgotten study dates, or other pressing issues that made them leave in the middle of their shifts. Many left without telling anyone. Because they were volunteers, such behavior was tolerated— unless it became too common.

"I don't have to do anything for fifteen minutes," he said.

Except find better music, she thought.

"I can look for her."

"Would you? Her home number's on the news log in the basement."

"No prob."

Marisa let go of the intercom, glanced at the digital clock on the board, and realized she was behind. She finished setting up the booth, then went downstairs. The pundits had already called Reagan's landslide, and Rob was sitting in front of CNN. He had three pencils in his thinning red hair, and his taped glasses had slid down his nose.

"Can I do my commentary this update?" he asked.

"No," she said. "I've got two live interviews, a phone connection, and too much information to report."

"But this is perfect. With them calling Reagan, I'd be timely."

She glanced at him. "What're you going to say?"

"You can read it."

"You know I can't." Rob's copy was always so messy it looked like hieroglyphics.

He leaned back in the ancient, squeaky office chair. "Okay. I have it boiled down to one minute. It's satire."

He said that because on her first newscast as news director, she hadn't been listening closely, and she had chewed him a new asshole for making up lies about Nancy Reagan. *It's a joke!* he had cried. *A joke!* Since then, he'd figured Marisa hadn't had a sense of humor.

"I'm doing a piece on why Sylvester Stallone should run in 1988. He's short, he's good-looking, he's powerful—"

"He can't enunciate," Joseph said, while he was typing.

"—Ah," Rob said. "But he can take orders just like Ronnie can. This is the era of the celluloid president. Imagine Stallone getting on the podium to the *Rocky* theme—"

"Do we have that in the library?" Marisa asked.

"I don't know," Rob said.

"Check. We'll run your commentary next hour, and when the time comes, you'll cue me to run that theme music. It'll work."

"Brilliant!" Rob said, and ran out the door. She grabbed more UPI copy.

"Brilliant," Joseph echoed. "You managed to make him forget he wanted to go on this time."

She shrugged. She'd been dealing with Rob for a long time. "Everybody upstairs," she said. She glanced at Channel Six's graphic of the races. Still no surprises. Thank heavens. She had too small a crew for surprises.

This newscast was brighter than the last. In addition to Councilwoman Bader, Senator George was supposed to show. He was always late, and Marisa made certain he wasn't billed in the intro. She followed her anchors upstairs, noted Kamal still at the reception desk, and told him to send in George when he showed. Kamal nodded.

Then the three of them went inside.

Blackburn was still a bit pale from his strange phone conversation—or perhaps it was the continuation of the Reagan Revolution that was making him ill. He certainly didn't like the way the country was going. None of them did. Hate mongering, talk of war, calling the Soviet Union the Evil Empire. For all of Rob's fun about the celluloid president, there was just enough truth in it—just enough continuation of the bad old policies—to make her nervous.

After Blackburn had cued her out, he disappeared from his booth, and she ran her newscast. Kamal buzzed her when Senator George arrived, and Naomi was positioning his mike as he sat down. No on-air glitches, even though the City Hall line dumped just after Douglas's update.

More bullets dodged. Three more newscasts to go. They'd

shut down at midnight, and everyone would go to the nearest bar, too wired to sleep.

Senator George raced off to his next interview without a goodbye. Joseph forgot his copy in the studio as usual, and Marisa cleaned up before going downstairs. Blackburn was in his booth on time, but his pallor had grown. Marisa was beginning to wonder if he was seriously ill. He put Mozart's *Requiem* on the turntable—just the Kyrie and the Lachrymosa —and stood.

Marisa opened the door to his booth. "You know, this is the strangest jazz show I've ever heard."

"Found Holly," he said, his voice flat.

She had forgotten. God, how could she forget all the time? It was as if the only part of the world that existed were the numbers, the voices, the 15-minute updates.

"Was she at home?" Marisa asked, even though she knew Holly hadn't been, not from the look on Blackburn's face.

"She was out back, in the parking lot, face down. Between two cars." His voice was rough. "She'd have frozen to death if I hadn't found her. I don't know how long she was out there."

"No more than an hour," Marisa said, knowing in these temperatures, Holly wouldn't have survived more than a few hours. They had been lucky.

"I called an ambulance."

"And the police?"

He nodded. The *Requiem* continued over the speakers, going past the announced "Lachrymosa."

"Shit," he said and slipped into the booth. Marisa followed. He was bent over a pile of LPs leaning up against the turntable.

"You know," she said. "You might want to go back to scheduled programming."

He shook his head. "The police said not to do anything different."

"The police came here?"

"They're probably still here."

Interviewing people. Getting in the way of her updates. She felt a tug—a pull she hadn't felt in a long time. The calls frightened her, and she liked Holly, but for ten years, Marisa had lived for the shows. They had to continue as well.

She left the booth without saying anything. The double doors closed behind her. Kamal was still at reception, looking flustered. A policeman, short and a bit stout, stood at the top of the stairs.

Marisa ignored him and ran down the stairs. Sure enough, three officers were in the newsroom, and no one was working.

"I'm sorry," she said, "but we have a newscast to put on."

One of the officers turned around. He was slender, with dark eyes and a sharp chin. He held his cap under his arm, revealing tousled black hair. "You must be Marisa Turner."

"Yes," she said. "Look, I am as worried about this as anyone, but—"

"I understand you took the first call."

"Yes, but—"

"When was this?"

She straightened. She wouldn't get sidelined. "I'll answer questions in a moment. But I need to keep order here too. You told Blackburn to proceed as if nothing were happening. The only way we can do that is to put on a newscast in—" she glanced at the clock "—forty minutes."

"I appreciate your problem, Ms. Turner, but—"

"No, I don't think you do. Just give me a moment, and then I'll talk to you." She gave instructions in rapid-fire, afraid that this officer would interrupt her, that the police would shut them down entirely. Joseph was to go over copy if she was gone; Naomi to double-check the studio; Rob to talk to Douglas at City Hall; otherwise everyone else should continue their jobs, make sure the updates were finished, and no stories were repeated. "And for godsakes, make sure Kamal knows the mayor is due at five after the hour."

They all nodded, even one of the officers, which made her realize just how strident her voice had become. She turned to the officer who had spoken to her.

"All right," she said. "Now I'll answer questions, but in the office, not here."

He raised an eyebrow, but followed her. The office wasn't really an office at all, but a series of desks placed at random in the concrete basement, along with boxes of old air check tapes, and file cabinets used as room dividers. The area was dark, the only illumination coming from the stair lights and the thin light from the newsroom. She hit a switch, and the fluorescents fluttered on. The place looked almost normal. There was never any daylight here. In the winter, she would enter the station in the dark and emerge in the dark, as if she were living a night that would never ever end.

"All right," she said, perching on the program manager's desk. "I got the first call at 7:55 and thought it was a prank. I asked Blackburn if he'd been getting calls like that, but he said no. We discussed it for a moment, thought it was too vague, and then I went back to work."

"Seven-fifty-five," the officer said. He was the only one who had followed her.

"Where are the others?" she asked, realizing that they were gone.

"Looking to see who else is in the building," he said. He was leaning against the music director's desk, his posture mimicking hers. "I hadn't realized it was so large."

"It used to be a warehouse." She extended her hand toward the boxes. "As you can see, we haven't really made good use of the space."

"Seven fifty-five," he said again. "You know this precisely?"

"Actually, Officer—" she paused, peered at him, and then frowned. "You realize you never properly introduced yourself."

His eyebrows went up again. She had never seen anyone do that in real life. She had always thought it a television affectation. "I did in the newsroom, but you weren't there yet."

She crossed her arms. "So…?"

"Guy Bergen. Detective Guy Bergen. You want my badge number?"

She shook her head. "Identification will do. How's Holly?"

"Unconscious, beginnings of frostbite. It'll take some time before we get a report."

"But you thought it worthy to talk with us about it?"

"Considering she was bashed over the head with a blunt object as yet undetermined, yes, I do." He crossed his arms as he said that. "How did you know it was seven fifty-five?"

"Seven fifty-five and thirty seconds, to be exact," she said. "And, even though I don't wear a watch and I have my back to the clock, I can tell you that it's now 9:21."

"No seconds?" he asked.

She shrugged. "I can't do seconds when my back is turned."

"How do you do minutes?"

"Every one counts when you're doing this kind of news-cast. We only have forty-five minutes to get the next show on the air, and it has to be interesting enough, and different enough to keep the regular listeners tuned in. It'd be easier if we expected a different audience every hour, but Blackburn's jazz show is popular—"

"I have no idea why," Bergen muttered. "It's depressing."

"—and it runs until midnight. The Arbitron's show that people don't tune out, and our own research has shown that people go out of their way to tune him in."

Bergen's gaze was baleful.

"He normally plays a bit more Charlie Parker. Some Ella. The dirges are new." She had no idea why she felt the need to explain herself.

"So, what did your caller say?"

She told him. She told him everything she could remember, from her call to Holly's. "I told her to call the police. The non-emergency number."

"She did. We logged it in," he said.

"Blackburn got another call."

"I know," Bergen said. "How many phone lines do you have?"

"Eight," she said, "all different numbers."

"Accessible from every phone?"

She nodded. "But the call wasn't internal."

"How do you know?"

"I was looking at the phone when I picked up. Line one was Douglas on hold at City Hall. Line two was Blackburn, talking to some listener. I picked up line three."

"Do the lines roll over?" Bergen asked.

"Yes," she said.

Blackburn was now playing Dixieland funeral music. It was a bit more upbeat, but heavy on the low brass. Bergen glanced at the overhead speakers. "He seems like a strange guy."

Marisa shrugged. "No stranger than the rest of us."

"Can you be sure it wasn't him on the line?"

Her smile was small. "I specialize in voices, officer."

"Detective," he said.

She ignored his correction. "I would have recognized his."

"Even if he had disguised it?"

"It's not that easy for a person to disguise his voice. Basic inflections remain the same." She glanced behind her at the clock. "Are we done?"

"You're not worried about your friend Holly?"

"Yes," she said. "But I can't do anything. And I have a job here."

"Would it matter if the station went off the air for the night?"

Her hands gripped the desktop. He didn't understand the daily struggle, the meetings, the requests for money. For the last ten years, her entire life had been organized around keeping the station on the air. To lose tonight, along with the publicity around Holly's attack, might be a blow that the station couldn't recover from.

"Yes," she said.

"Hmm." He picked up a pencil, one of the gimmes a volunteer had designed. It had the station's call letters on it and last spring's fundraising slogan: *The Aural Majority.*

Marisa shifted. She didn't know why she was waiting for him to excuse her, as if she were a student facing the principal. "Are other stations getting these calls?" she asked.

"No," he said.

"The TV stations?"

"No."

"The newspapers?"

"No."

"The campaigns? The political offices?"

"No."

"Just us?"

He nodded.

"And you think the calls represent a real threat now that Holly was attacked?"

"Don't you?"

She didn't know. "We get crank calls a lot."

"And people attacked in your parking lot?"

"Not so much."

He frowned at her, apparently thinking she was joking. She wasn't.

"It's not a good neighborhood. We had a lot of trouble a year ago when we first moved into the building. Most of our volunteers are cautious now, but we still have the occasional mugging."

He was watching her more intently than anyone had in a long time. Did he think she was lying? Making excuses? Maybe she was. She could feel the clock ticking behind her, the precious seconds disappearing as they talked.

"Is that what you think this is? A mugging? Coincidentally timed with a crank call?"

"I don't think anything," she said, venturing another look at the clock behind her. It was 9:35, just as she suspected it was. Less than a half hour to make sure the newscast went on without a hitch. "I've been concentrating on work."

"I need to talk to your people."

"Fine," she said. "As long as it's one at a time, and not between 9:55 and 10:20."

"I hope to be done by then." He set the pencil down. "A lot of important people come through here on election night, don't they?"

She froze. No wonder the police had come in full force. "Yes."

"Who do you have lined up for the rest of the night?"

She gave him a verbal list, thinking about the possible disaster as she did so: five state representatives, a congressman, a few more city council people, and the mayor.

"The governor often comes here, doesn't he?"

Her hands were cold. "Only if he wins. He knows he has a strong constituency among our listeners."

"I'm going to stay here for a while," he said. "Then when I go, I'll be leaving a few of my men in the station and the parking lot."

"There's more going on than a few calls and a woman getting mugged, isn't there?" Marisa asked softly.

He stared at her for a moment, as if he were judging whether or not he could tell her this next. Finally, he said, "Friends of cranks usually don't call the police with warnings."

The chill she had been feeling got deeper. "You have no idea about the intended target?"

"None," he said. "Only that whatever will happen will happen here, tonight."

"Maybe Holly scared the person off."

"Maybe," he said. "Or maybe she knew him."

It was 9:45. Marisa could feel it without even looking at the clock. She had to check on the broadcast. "Do you think that person is here, now?"

"Possibly."

"Someone working here?"

"You don't exactly have tight security."

"We have no security," she said. "But we do have the benefit of only one door."

"I'd like to check storage areas and offices," he said.

"I'll give you my keys." She got up and headed back to the newsroom. It was a mass of chaos: Joseph sitting on top of the desk, calling out stories; Rob on the phone, one hand pressed against his ear so that he could hear the person on the other end; Naomi scanning copy; and two volunteers typing frantically. The UPI machine was beeping, some analyst on CBS was talking about the continuation of the Reagan Revolution, and Channel Six was declaring the governor a winner.

Marisa dug in her purse and found her wad of keys.

"Great security," Bergen said.

"We're a listener-sponsored station," she said. "Our mandate makes us open to the public."

"And theft."

She shook her head. "If we had anything to steal, the station manager would have sold it for parts a long time ago."

He clutched the keys in his hand. "Care to show me which goes where?"

She glanced at the newsroom. "Love to, but can't."

He nodded and disappeared. She took the phone from Rob, turned away from him, and said into the receiver, "Is anyone at the governor's?"

"D-Douglas," one of the rookie volunteers answered, sounding as if he were going to pee his pants at any moment.

"He left City Hall?"

"Yes, ma'am."

"Excellent." She put her hand over the mouthpiece. "Tape any incoming calls. Douglas should be calling with Channel Six announcing." She moved her hand. "Who's handling the returns at City Hall?"

"I-I am."

Damn. She hated being understaffed. "All right. You're doing the 10:05 update. Make sure you have the numbers written down on a piece of paper, and don't worry about sounding good. This is live radio. You're going to hold from now until we go on the air."

"Okay," the rookie said.

Marisa punched the hold button and put the receiver down. "Who was that?" she asked Rob.

He shrugged. They'd have to wing it at 10:05. "Say,

Marisa," he said softly, leaning toward her, "how long are the cops gonna be here?"

"Until we're done, I guess." She frowned. She didn't know what Rob was worried about. There were too many old hippies at the station for anyone to talk about his side business. No one would narc. "You're going to have to talk to them."

"Can you put it off?"

"I don't think so. But you probably can. Just look busy all the time."

He grinned. "I'm good at that."

She smiled back. "I know." Then she turned to Joseph. "Is the studio set up?"

"Naomi was supposed to do that."

Marisa raised her eyebrows in query at Naomi. Naomi cursed, which Marisa took for a no. Marisa hurried up the stairs. One cop sat near Kamal at the desk. Kamal was going over some other copy—finally learning to look busy.

Through the small square windows that looked out onto the street, Marisa saw another cop, blowing on his gloved hands and rocking from foot to foot. It was cold out there. Winter had come early this year. Holly probably would have frozen to death a few feet away from them all. Marisa let that thought go in. Holly. Her friend. A woman she'd worked with for years and years. A woman she'd relied on. Marisa would have felt terrible if she died. Marisa already felt awful that she had been hurt.

Marisa allowed herself a small shudder and then hurried into the studio. She certainly hoped there wasn't a nut around the station. She hoped she had been right—that it was a simple mugging. She glanced through glass at Blackburn, who was putting another record on the turntable. The Dixieland had segued back into some more dirges, mixed with choral requiems more suited to the morning classical shows than the jazz programs. He didn't see her stare.

Was Bergen right? Could Blackburn have done something like that? Her sense of him was that he didn't have a violent bone in him. She trusted those senses, always had.

She set up the studio, checked the reel-to-reel inside the booth, and got the cart ready. She didn't have time for any other checks, even though all five microphones would be used, as well as the phone.

It was 9:55. She ran downstairs, hoping that her crew was as good as she thought they were. As she stepped into the newsroom, the phone rang.

Joseph picked it up, and his mouth immediately went slack.

"Get Bergen," Marisa said to one of the volunteers as she pressed the record button on the phone machine. Then she slowly punched the same phone line that Joseph was on, careful to shut off her receiver before she picked up.

"...politics," the same strange nasal male voice was saying. "It kills."

And then he hung up. Joseph glanced at her across the room. His skin was ashen.

Marisa glanced at the clock. 9:59. Joseph followed her gaze. They swore in unison, and grabbed their materials. "Tell Bergen we've got tape," she yelled to one of the rookie volunteers as she sprinted up the stairs.

Two congressmen stood beside the police at the door. They were looking serious in their suits.

"Get them in the studio," she yelled at Kamal as she passed. She ran through both sets of doors, and landed in her chair as Blackburn introduced the update. She punched the music cart as she potted it up, then she slipped on her headphones, nodding at the precise moments for her anchors to begin their lead-ins.

They did it flawlessly, despite Joseph's continued paleness and Kamal's loud banging as he got the congressmen settled. Naomi signaled for quiet, and finally Kamal left the room.

Marisa was halfway through the phone interview with the rookie at City Hall (named David Davis. She had to remind herself to give rookies with weird names on-air names. No one would believe this one) when Bergen poked his head in the door.

"Not now," she said.

Naomi sliced a finger across her neck, meaning that she had no more questions for the rookie.

"I hear you got a tape of the caller," Bergen said.

Marisa shut off the phone pot, and brought up the congressmen's mike. She waited to hear their hellos to Joseph and Naomi before answering Bergen. "It's on the machine attached to the phone marked ***2 in the newsroom."

"Great," he said, and let himself out.

Too late, she remembered that Rob was supposed to do his commentary this hour. Where had he gone to? He should have come up the stairs with them. Not that it mattered. She didn't have the theme music from *Rocky* cued up anyway.

The congressmen finished as Kamal was leading two

county commissioners into the studio. There were some loud greetings, which she managed to pot down, and one hefty thump against the mike table which probably sent listeners bouncing out of their chairs. Then the interviews continued.

At fourteen after, Marisa gave them the signal to wind down. They did—Joseph managing some cogent analysis of the tight 4th District city council race—and Marisa brought up the music. She shut off all the mikes, and said, "We're off."

The anchors stood, spoke to the politicians still in the room, while Marisa leaned back in her chair. She hadn't done an engineering stint like that in a long time. She was covered in sweat. The 11 o'clock update would be the crucial one: most of the votes that would be counted this night would be in, and it would be pretty clear where the races would end up. The midnight report would simply be a wrap-up. If she could keep 11 o'clock on track, everything would be fine.

She left the studio to find Bergen waiting for her. He took her arm and led her toward the mailroom in the back.

"Hey," she said. "I've got to—"

"Did you listen to that tape?"

"I only heard the last few seconds, then I had to come up here."

"It was filled with a lot of invective, some of it personal toward the person on the phone. Who answered?"

"Joseph," she said. She was cold again.

"He works for the university, doesn't he?"

"The medical school," she said.

"He was told that his history would come out, if he weren't careful, and that a man like him should know how dangerous political opinions were. A man who acted on them often got killed."

Marisa frowned. "You're kidding."

Bergen shook his head. "I want you to listen. There's a lot of voice there. I want to see if you can identify it."

"Let's see if the entire newsroom can. A dozen ears are better than mine," she said.

She led him into the music library, filled with albums stacked alphabetically by category, and beginning to fill with CDs. More speakers hung on the walls. Now Blackburn was playing Gregorian chant, which sounded even more funereal than the dirges he had played earlier. She stepped around a pile of boxes and went down the back stairs. Bergen followed.

She didn't say anything to him as they went past the dark offices into the newsroom. She went to the reel-to-reel, flicked the broadcast switch, rewound the eighth of an inch of tape, then turned to her people.

"All right," she said. "If any of you even think you recognize this voice, speak out."

Bergen shook his head slightly, then sighed. He might have had a system in which this would go slowly, but she didn't have time for it. She didn't have time for anything.

Marisa hit "play." The nasal voice, sounding even tinnier filtered through the phone line and the tape, was speaking.

...know you were in Berkeley. Heard you preferred LSD. What would the University say if they knew one of their prime researchers was a big dope fiend? The war on drugs has heated up, my friend, and people go to jail for a little Mary Jane in their big, beautiful houses. Like the stuff you scored a few weeks ago.

Joseph's face was red.

...You of all people should know that politics is personal, and now it's going against you. Conservative and difficult. Hell, even your associations at the station could get you killed. But you always knew that, didn't you? From the sixties to the eighties, the only uniform thing about politics: it kills.

Beads of sweat stood out on Joseph's forehead. Marisa felt chills go through her. Bergen was watching all of them, but other than Joseph, no one else looked deeply distressed. They were all clearly disturbed by the voice.

"Anyone?" Marisa asked.

No one responded, although several people looked surreptitiously at Joseph. Bergen's mouth was a thin line. "I've already talked to Dr. Hecht. If anyone else wants to speak with me in private, I'd be willing to listen."

Then he reached down and removed the tape from the reel. He held it up to Marisa. "You don't mind," he said, and it wasn't a question.

"I was going to offer it myself," she said.

His smile was small. Then he left the newsroom, but she had a hunch he hadn't gone very far.

She shook out her shoulders, feeling the tension, hearing her back crack. She glanced at Channel Six, saw how their stats had changed, wondered if this night was ever going to end. Then she turned to the UPI machine.

Rob put a hand on her arm. "We missed my commentary."

"I know."

"I couldn't find the *Rocky* theme."

"Did you ask for help?"

"Yeah. I don't think we have it."

She knew they did. She had used it on a newscast

before. "It's—" she started to explain, then remembered she was dealing with Rob. He couldn't find anything in the music library. She had known better than to send him. "I'll get it."

He followed her across the dark offices and up the stairs like a lost puppy. They had done this so many times over the years that she wondered why she hadn't gotten the album herself. It was a sign of how distracted she was, how over-worked she felt, just how much strain she was under on this long, long night.

The soundtracks were at the end of the second aisle. She walked down it, following the alphabet. The *Rocky* album was extended slightly, as if someone had pulled it out, and then decided against it.

She grabbed it and turned. Rob was pressed against her. He had a strange look in his eyes. She felt a slight frisson of fear. She had never seen him quite like this.

He put a finger to his lips, then glanced around. "I know who's making those calls," he whispered. "He's been making them to me at home."

Marisa let out an exasperated breath. "Then tell Bergen."

"I can't!" Rob ran a hand through his hair. "It's Tim, a guy I met when I was in Mexico. He's been supplying me."

Marisa's eyes narrowed. "What did you do?"

"Nothing."

"People don't harass other people for nothing."

"I owe him money." Rob owed everyone money. It was one of his charms. He lived on a meager budget and supplemented it by selling drugs to his friends, writing term papers for college students, and occasional articles for the independent weeklies in town. The rest of the time, he volunteered at the station.

"How much money?" Marisa said.

"Not enough for him to do this!"

"How'd he know about Joseph?"

"Tim lived with me for a while. He knows about the station." And everyone in it, she supposed. Rob was a good, and sometimes naive, storyteller. She never told him secrets because he blabbed them, just like he blabbed about his own illegal dealings.

She asked, "Did this Tim hit Holly?"

"Probably." Rob winced. "He came after me a couple of times."

She remembered. Two weeks ago, Rob had come in covered with bruises. A month before that, he'd had a black eye. He hadn't explained either incident, but he had let Joseph look him over.

"You think he's out back?"

"Not with the cops here. Maybe not even after hitting her. He's not exactly the courageous type."

She stared at Rob for a moment. "So why'd he call again?"

"So I'd know. There are other ways to hurt my friends."

She felt her mouth tighten. "You tell Bergen, or I will."

"He'll arrest me."

"Probably."

"I can't afford to be arrested."

"You can't afford to be killed."

Rob bit his lower lip. "Can it wait until I finished my commentary?"

He wasn't going to say a word to Bergen. She knew it from

the look on his face. Rob would give his commentary and then he would sneak out the door when no one was looking, and either make good his escape, or die in the snow like Holly nearly did.

"Sure," Marisa said. "Do your commentary. You're on at 11."

He smiled at her. "Thanks," he said. "I knew I could count on you."

"I'm a regular brick," she said dryly and took the record into the booth. It took her a few minutes to cue up the theme, to find the right selection to play beneath one minute of commentary. It took her longer than usual because her hands were shaking.

It was an unspoken rule of the station: no squealing. There were draft dodgers still wanted by the federal government. There were minor drug dealers, like Rob, and minor drug users, like Joseph. There were members of the SDS and the Weather Underground who had foresworn violence in their old age, but still had outstanding warrants. No one spoke of it, except in whispers. Everyone figured people's business was their own. Current crimes were victimless. Past crimes were past. Some even saw volunteering at the station as community service, a form of non-government-regulated atonement.

She bowed her head and put her shaking hand over her eyes. If Rob knew the guy behind the threats, and the police thought the threats credible enough to station people here on a crazy night like election night, then Rob was in danger. Holly had already been hurt. Rob wasn't going to report this. But Marisa could.

And she had until 11:15 to do so.

"Dammit," she whispered.

She wouldn't lose her job, but she would lose her credibility, with her friends. This was the last bastion of left-wing idealism, and the rules were simple: everyone had a right to live his own life his way; and no one narced. Not ever.

She double-checked the studio, then went back downstairs. Her mind was so far away from the election that she wasn't sure she would ever be able to think about it again.

If Rob died because she remained quiet, she wouldn't be able to live herself.

Rob was a gentle man, one who couldn't survive prison. She knew it, and she knew with the Reagan Administration's tough drug laws, Rob probably wouldn't stand a chance of going free. He was the kind of person the Feds loved to make an example of.

But Bergen wasn't a Fed. And prison wasn't as bad as dying. Nothing was. This Tim had already shown he didn't care about the lives of Rob's friends. He had nearly killed Holly, and he had threatened Joseph.

Marisa's stomach turned. She loved this place. She loved it because it wasn't just a radio station. It was, in its own way, home. It survived on spit and polish and ideals. And the ideals were important, they were something that gave the station its lifeblood. Listeners pledged money because they heard news they didn't hear on any other station, music they didn't know existed, interviews with people who couldn't get airtime anywhere else. All because of the lack of commercial support, and a driving vision that said even the smallest voice had to be heard.

She let herself out of the studio, and of course, Bergen was there, waiting for her. All her adult life, she had hated cops, feared them and hadn't trusted them. They were establishment, conservative, pigs. They didn't get it, and they never would.

His gaze met hers. He was smarter than she wanted him to be, and he was her age. He understood the arguments, even though he had chosen the other side.

"What do you know?" he asked.

Son of a bitch. She never could hide anything. She stared back at him. They both knew his question was valid. The remaining question was whether or not she'd lie to him—as her training demanded. As Rob had thought she would.

Was it Freud or Plato who said that mankind had to voluntarily give up cherished freedoms to have the protection provided by society? And society itself placed certain demands, among them the right to live without threat.

Threat.

"Marisa?" he asked.

She felt herself bristle at his use of her first name. She hadn't given him permission to do so. For a moment, that seemed like excuse enough to push past him and go down the stairs.

But something wouldn't let her do it. Something more fundamental than elusive ideals and politicized views of the police.

"Come with me," she said. She led him into the mailroom, flicked on the light, and closed the door. She had never been in this room at night. The light was thin, the flyers that stuck out of the mail holes looking like sticks in the semi-darkness.

The saggy couch looked even more old and uncomfortable than it did during the day.

Bergen stood at attention, his hands clasped behind his back. His features were impassive.

"You have to promise me," she said, "that you'll keep this conversation private."

"If I can."

"That's not a promise."

"It's the best I can do," he said.

She knew that. She knew it, but she didn't want to give him any quarter at all. She hadn't realized how hard this would be.

"I'm going to tell you something that I'm not supposed to tell you, that I would never tell you under any other circumstances."

"All right." He hadn't moved, but he sounded intrigued.

"I want you to promise me you'll do everything you can to protect the person I'm going to tell you about—and if you don't, I swear, the police department has never heard of negative press, not like what I can deliver."

He smiled. "A threat?"

She shook her head, even though she was lying. God, she was afraid of what he'd do. Had all her years in the counter-culture brought her to this? An unwillingness to use the very services that most people trusted?

"Rob," she said, "has a commentary at 11. I want you to let him finish it. I don't want you to do anything until we go off the air."

"All right." He was watching her carefully. She knew he was confused.

"And then I don't want you to do anything in front of my staff. In private only, or I swear I—"

"I understand the threat," he said, that hint of a smile peeking out again.

She licked her lips. Her stomach was jumping. She hadn't been this unsure of herself since she was what? Nineteen? "Rob occasionally sells cocaine. In small amounts, to friends only. He used to only handle marijuana, but the eighties—"

"I know," Bergen said.

"Small amounts. Nothing large. And those are the only drugs he ever touches."

"All right."

"The calls are coming from a supplier of his." She closed her eyes. "Rob owes him money."

She opened her eyes again. Bergen was watching her.

"Did he give you a name?"

"Just the first name," she said.

Bergen stared at her as if she were lying. She swallowed. This wasn't going the way she wanted it to.

"Rob never has any money. It's not how he lives. The supplier knows this, but he's trying to intimidate it out of him. Tonight's an escalation. I think this has probably been going on a long time—" and as she said that, she thought of how haggard Rob had looked lately, how unwilling he had been to stay around and chat "—and the supplier's getting desperate."

"Or maybe he owes someone else money and is leaning on Rob."

She nodded. "Anyway, he's targeting the station because we're Rob's friends. We're his family."

"Holly was a warning."

"I think so."

"You know I'll have to take Rob in, probably arrest him."

"I know," she said. "But can't you give him some kind of immunity if he talks? He's not a big fish."

"Do you think your friend Rob will tell on his friends?"

"His friends wouldn't try to kill someone," she said. "Remind him of that."

Her heart was pounding and she was sweating as if she had just gotten off the air.

"I'll wait," Bergen said, "until 11:15, and then I'll deal with Rob. I'll do what I can for him. It'll go easier if he works with me. Can you tell him that?"

She shook her head. "I shouldn't have talked to you. He said he was going to, but he wouldn't. I know. He would have disappeared after his commentary, and I was afraid…" Her voice broke. She ran a hand over her face.

"You were afraid they'd kill him," Bergen said softly.

She nodded, her hand still over her face. Tears threatened.

She was emotional because of stress. That was all. She made herself take a deep breath and the shaky feeling eased.

"You were right," Bergen said. "You—"

"Don't tell me I did the right thing." She let her hand drop. "You don't know what this will mean."

"I do." He spoke softly. "It means your friend Rob will live."

THE ELEVEN O'CLOCK update went on without a hitch—a miracle, Marisa felt, considering the way her hands shook and her stomach jumped. She yelled at Kamal when he came in to say that there were two uninvited Independent candidates in the foyer, and then immediately apologized, and told him to keep them there: she would interview them after the update.

All through the update, she couldn't look at Rob. He had asked her to keep things quiet, and she hadn't. She had never done anything like this, never stepped outside the community before, but she knew that it was right. She knew it, and she knew that Rob would be the one who would never forgive her.

His commentary was wry and funny, his Stallone impression dead-on, his prediction of the fate of the Presidency chilling at its core. With the *Rocky* theme music playing beneath it and the deep certainty in his voice, the commentary was the highlight of the entire evening—something so profound and dangerous it didn't belong on a local listener-sponsored station. It belonged on a national network, provoking attention from all over the country.

How could someone so smart be so stupid? How could he

see cultural patterns so clearly and lampoon them so well and not be able to see how his own problems would destroy the tiny culture he was a part of? How could he risk his life for some money and a few ounces of powder?

Perhaps he hadn't. Perhaps he had told her precisely because he knew she was the responsible one, because he knew that she would go to Bergen and do it in the right way. He didn't tell Joseph, who would have commiserated, nor did he tell Naomi, who could have given him legal advice. He told Marisa, who had no time to listen and who would protect the station at all costs.

At the end of the update, as she was potting up the outro music, her gaze met Rob's. He gave her a small smile. She gave him a thumbs up.

And that was the last she saw of him that night.

She stayed in the booth until 11:30, interviewing the two Independents, then setting up the studio for the last update at midnight. By the time she came out, with a tape for one of the volunteers to cut, both Bergen and Rob were long gone.

Only Kamal had seen them leave together, and he was too new to know how strange that was. Marisa didn't have time to ask questions, nor did she want to: she didn't want to draw attention to the strangeness of it all.

Her stomach was acid, her mind numb. She cobbled the final update together—most of the election statistics were the same. There would be no more real news until morning—and she organized the final tapes from City Hall. The stringers were straggling in from their various assignments: they'd be up until two or three a.m. preparing stories for the following morning's broadcasts. Her regular writers were finishing their stories. Joseph was picking through the best of the commentary for one more newscast.

"Rob disappeared fast," he said as Marisa came into the newsroom.

"Yeah," she said, and turned her attention to sorting the last of the UPI copy. CNN was interviewing some shrill election official from a Western state, upset that several of the major markets announced Reagan as a landslide winner two hours before the Western polls closed. That was a good story, and one she would have assigned someone for the next day, but she didn't have the energy or the heart.

The midnight update wasn't as good as the eleven, but it had more meat. The governor showed up for one of his election night surprise visits—a tradition, he told her as he shook her hand on the way out—and the last interview, with one of the state's U.S. senators had a few surprises in it that would make the national news—if Marisa could find someone to cut and wrap it before six a.m. Maybe the promise of real money would do it.

She staggered out of the booth, after clearing the carts and tapes and debris from the hectic night. Kamal had left reception, and the midnight-to-six rock-and-roll DJ was already in his booth, playing "Jonny B. Goode." Blackburn was in the music library putting away his dirges. He would join the crew, as he always did, for the election night post-game analysis at Tuft's Tavern down the street.

As she passed the reception desk, the phone rang. A chill ran down her back. What if she had been wrong? What if Rob had been wrong? What if he hadn't known who that voice belonged to?

She set down the pile of materials she was carrying, and punched the line, giving the station's call letters in a no-nonsense voice.

"I'm calling for Marisa ..."

"This is," she said. The voice was different, but familiar. She had heard it just recently. It was—

"Detective Bergen. I thought I'd give you an update."

"Okay." She sat on the edge of the desk. Joseph came up the stairs and looked at her curiously. She pointed to the items on the desk and mimed carrying them. He did, disappearing downstairs again. All the while, Detective Bergen was talking.

"We have a man named Tim Ibarra in custody, and our men found enough drugs in his apartment to build a large case against him. We also found some evidence that will lead to a few other arrests."

"Rob?" she asked.

"Is fine. He called an attorney, and he'll be out within a few hours. We're going to charge him, but recommend leniency— probation and community service—if he testifies against Ibarra. He did give us the name, so I trust he'll cooperate."

He probably gave the name because she had already given part of it. Marisa said nothing. For the first time that night, she had no idea what to say.

"That's the best I could do," Bergen said. "I just wanted you to know."

"I appreciate it," she said.

There was silence on the other end for a long moment. She wasn't sure if she should have hung up. Then Bergen said, "His commentary was brilliant."

"Yes," she said. "Yes, it was."

"I voted for Reagan."

"I figured."

"Your friend made me wonder if I should have, if I was voting for a man or an image."

"Rob's good at that."

"Maybe this will scare him a little," Bergen said. "Turn him around. Make him use his talents for a wider audience."

"Maybe," she said.

"But you don't think so."

"Rob's living a lifestyle only a few people believe in any more. It's political for him. Do you understand that?"

"Yes," Bergen said. "It's political for all of you, for all your pretense at objectivity."

She smiled, glad he couldn't see her. The station always thought that was its own little secret. "I didn't expect your call, detective. Thanks."

"No," he said quietly. "I know how difficult it is to be out of touch with the people around you. I appreciate you stepping away, for just that moment, to do this thing."

He had understood what it cost her then. Her assessment of him hadn't been wrong. He knew, and he valued it. Somehow that made things a little better.

She hung up and went downstairs. Naomi was putting on her coat. Joseph was frowning.

"You know they arrested Rob tonight?"

"Yes," Marisa said. "I was just talking to the detective. Seems Rob knew the caller. The man was threatening him. The detective isn't interested in Rob. He wants the connections."

"That's what Rob said." Naomi pulled on her mittens. "He called while you were upstairs."

"How is he?" Marisa asked.

"Scared," Naomi said, "I'm not a criminal attorney, but I can protect Rob's butt tonight. Tomorrow, I'm going to get one of the best guys in the state to work on his case, pro bono."

"You can do that?" Joseph asked.

"No, but I know a judge who owes me one." Naomi tugged on her stocking cap and looked at Marisa. "Rob had a message for you."

Marisa froze.

"He wanted me to tell you that you did the best work of your life tonight."

Marisa's knees gave out. She sat in a metal folding chair, listening to it creak beneath her. "It was just an election night," she said.

"The world changes on election night," Joseph said with a rueful smile. "I learned that twenty years ago."

"Me, too." Naomi grabbed her briefcase. She looked like a cross between a student and a lawyer. "I'll meet you guys at Tuft's with news." And then she left.

Marisa got the one of the remaining volunteers to cut the governor's tape, and sent her to Booth Two to work.

Joseph waited for Marisa, slapping his gloves against his hands. "You turned Rob in, didn't you?" he asked.

Marisa swallowed. She nodded.

He stared at her for a long moment, his dark eyes appraising. "We don't go to cops."

"The guy was threatening Rob."

"Rob would have handled it."

"Rob?"

Joseph nodded. "Rob's handled things before."

"Like this? The guy nearly killed Holly."

"Not intentionally."

Marisa was shaking. "Yes, intentionally. Don't you understand? He would have hurt Rob. He probably would have hurt you."

"Don't you understand?" Joseph asked, grabbing his coat and throwing it over his arm. "That's how these guys work. They threaten until someone caves. You caved."

"I got him locked up."

"At what cost? Rob? You think he'll get off, now that Ronnie's got a new term?"

"Bergen promised me—"

"Bergen?" Joseph asked. "You believed a cop?"

She took a deep breath, then let it out slowly. "Yes."

Joseph slung his coat over his shoulders. "You talk the talk, but when it comes time to walk the walk, you're just like the rest of them. You have no clue what it means to be radical."

"What does it mean?" she asked. "Living in a nice house near the university? Working a salaried job?"

"I do medical research."

"Yeah, and you make a fortune, and you volunteer here to salve your conscience. Or is it so that you can score some dope on the side? Is that what's bugging you?"

His eyes narrowed. "I did my time in the trenches, girl. And I'd never narc on a friend."

"Even if the friend died because of your silence?"

"Even if the friend died."

She was breathing hard. Their faces were only an inch apart. "Now I know why you're in medical research, Dr. Hecht. No one would trust you to handle patients."

"I do what's right," he said.

"Do you?" she asked.

"More than you'll ever know," he said and left.

"That was charming." Blackburn was standing in the darkness just outside the newsroom door. He let himself in. He had his coat on too. "Guess he's not waiting for the rest of us."

"You still want to go?" she asked. "With a narc like me?"

"Narc, hell," he said. "You could use a drink."

He grabbed her coat off the rack, and held it out to her.

"Twenty years ago," he said, "it seemed so easy. And sometimes it still does. But sometimes..." He shook his head. "...the rules—or the anti-rules—don't give you any solutions at all. Just questions."

She looked at him.

He shrugged. "It's not Berkeley in '64. Or anywhere in '68. Or '72. It's 1984. Big Brother year."

"And I guess Big Brother has got to me."

Blackburn shook his head. "You just recognized what Dylan always knew. The times are still a-changing."

"You're not mad at me?"

"For saving Rob? Maybe. I always thought he was a prick." She felt herself smile. "For talking to Bergen."

"I don't see the world in black and white," Blackburn said.

"Then what were the dirges?" she asked.

His gaze met hers. His eyes were a vivid, and sad, blue. "Recognition," he said.

"Of?"

"The fact that the world is a place that I don't have a lot of control over." He sighed. "But you took control tonight. Maybe that's what pissed off Joseph."

"I went to the Establishment."

"Like it or not, Joseph is Establishment too. He just doesn't realize it."

She shook her head. "It's not that easy."

"It's not supposed to be." Blackburn picked up her purse and held it out to her. "Tufts?"

She took the coat. It was thin, cloth, bought used, and gave her little protection against the cold. She sacrificed a lot to be here. She just hadn't been willing to sacrifice Rob.

Maybe one day she'd tell Joseph that.

Maybe one day, he'd understand.

"Tuft's," she said. "On one condition."

"Name it," Blackburn said.

"Promise not to play another dirge ever again."

Blackburn grinned. "Can't. Reagan can only serve two terms. It's the law."

"Didn't think you believed in the law," she said.

"Only when it suits me," he said and winked. "And sometimes it suits me just fine.